*Paul
Prin*

This special signed edition is limited to
500 numbered copies and 26 lettered copies.

This is copy 362

Dating Secrets
of the Dead

Dating Secrets of the Dead

David Prill

Subterranean Press • 2003

Contents

DATING SECRETS OF THE DEAD

Hey Jerry, there's that new girl.

Oh yes. Her name's Caroline May Ames. She's a swell kid.

Why? Do you know her?

Not very well, Bud. I wish I did.

I don't know what it is, but there's something about her you like.

Well, she always looks nice for one thing.

They all look nice, at first...

•

Jerry hadn't had a date in an eternity. He didn't know why. They had dressed him so stylishly. His black dress shoes had such a sheen to them. His wispy brown hair was trimmed and combed. His cheeks had a ruddy, outdoorsy hue. His fingernails had once been nicely manicured — now they had grown long. Too long.

Maybe that was it. Maybe his uncut fingernails were turning off the girls.

No, it had to be more than that.

All in all, I look pretty sharp, he thought.

Then maybe it's my personality or personal habits.

I'm soft-spoken—my breath would hardly fog a mirror.

Polite. To a fault.

Interesting experiences to share. Absolutely. My life review was a gripping melodrama.

Jerry didn't want to face rejection again, but he did like that new girl, Caroline May Ames. They had exchanged small talk once before, the day she arrived. They were in the same row, after all. She was so pretty. Her white dress had ivory beads and lace. Her blonde hair cascaded comfortably over her shoulders. She had such a peaceful look on her face.

He called for her.

Hi, Caroline. This is Jerry.

Oh hi, Jerry.

I was wondering, Caroline, if you want to go out with me tonight?

Tonight? I'm sorry, I can't, Jerry. I already have a date for tonight. Why don't you call some other time?

Oh, okay. Thanks anyway, Caroline. Bye.

Goodbye, Jerry.

Strike out, Jerry thought, feeling dejected. Didn't she like him? She acted like she did. Then why didn't she want to go out with him?

He decided to ask Bud about it. Bud had been around longer than Jerry, and always seemed to have good advice to share.

…so I don't know what happened. I asked Caroline for a date, and she turned me down flat.

How long did the conversation last?

Not long. A minute or so.

That's good. Your call shouldn't go on for hours. That's a pretty sensible attitude. When did you ask her to go out with you?

Tonight.

There's your problem. Be sure not to wait until the last minute to ask a girl for a date. It's no compliment to any girl to call her so late that she thinks she's the last resort.

I never thought of that. Thanks a lot, Bud.

Glad to help, fella.

Jerry tried again the next day.

Hi, Caroline, this is Jerry.

Hi, Jerry.

Caroline, uh, I don't suppose you'd want to go out with me sometime.

Oh, I suppose we could. Call me sometime.

That was better. A real step in the right direction.

He told Bud about his success.

That's great, Jerry. When are you two going out, then?

Uh, we didn't exactly set a day.

How did you ask her?

Jerry told him.

Don't ask a girl out in a backhanded way that makes her feel uncomfortable. It's a mark of your insecurity, too. And one other tip: Don't ask a girl if she is busy on a certain night. That puts her on the spot.

Boy, this is more complicated than I thought, Jerry mused. *So how should I ask her then?*

David Prill

Think of something to do that she might like. Don't leave it entirely up to her. Suggest two or three activities, and see how she responds. Perhaps go out with a group of friends.

There's a skating party on Friday. Maybe Caroline would want to do that.

Now you've got the hang of it.

He called for Caroline again.

Hi, Jerry.

Hi, Caroline. Say, the gang is going to a skating party on Friday. I was wondering if you'd want to go with me. We'd have to leave early, but we'd get back by eleven. Or else we could spend the evening watching the flesh rot off our bones. We'd get back later if we did that.

Gee, Jerry, the skating party sounds like loads of fun. I'd love to go.

Great. I'll come for you around six.

Jerry was smart. He kept a date calendar, and checked it before asking Caroline to the party. Not a bad idea.

Good boy! Bud congratulated Jerry when told of his success with Caroline. *I wish I could go to the skating party but I told my folks I'd spend the evening with them. They don't get out much anymore.*

I really appreciate your help, said Jerry. *I just wish I could take you with me!*

Jerry was joshing Bud, but it was true. His friend knew the proper habit patterns, and what it took to be popular.

The days leading up to his date with Caroline seemed to crawl and creep. Throughout the week Jerry quizzed Bud on how he should behave on his date, what to say, what a girl expects. Finally, the weekend rolled in, and Jerry grew stiff with anticipation.

Wardrobe. Jerry decided to wear what he had on. His dark suit. It made him look more mature. A few holes, hardly noticeable, some mild staining in the crotch area, but Caroline would understand. She was that kind of girl.

A few minutes before six Jerry showed up where Caroline lived. He didn't need Bud to tell him the importance of promptness. He wanted to make a good impression on her folks, too.

Her parents were side by side when he arrived.

Good evening, Mr. and Mrs. Ames. I'm Jerry Weathers, Caroline's friend.

Even though they were Midwestern stoic, Jerry felt at ease with her mom and dad. There wasn't enough left of them to make trouble.

Jerry, how nice to see you.

Caroline.

She looked wonderful. White dress. Beads. Blonde hair. Shoulders. A portrayal of peace on her face.

Hi, Caroline. You look so natural.

Thanks. How nice of you to notice. She addressed her parents. *We should be back from the skating party by eleven.*

There is no magic formula about when to come home from a date. The hour Jerry and Caroline would return was decided by where they were going on their date, whether tomorrow is a school day, how many dates she has had recently, and so forth.

I'll take good care of her, Mr. and Mrs. Ames, said Jerry. *Good night.*

'Night, Mom and Dad. Don't wait up for us.

David Prill

As they met up with the gang for the skating party, Jerry felt relaxed and sociable. It had helped knowing Caroline, even just a little, before they went on their first date. Jerry had been on blind dates before. Most of them were dumb and mute, too, and then there was that headless girl. A midway-ride mishap, he had overheard during her interment. She was fun, but not really Jerry's type.

The skating party. It seemed unreal, that's how entranced he was with Caroline.

He felt light on his feet, Dead Astaire, his skate blades cutting into the dark sheet on the pond. They skated in a long loop, hand in hand. Caroline's hand was colder than hell. He tried warming it up with his own, but it didn't seem to help much.

As they skated beneath the festering full moon, they seemed to get into a rhythm with each other, carried away with the dance. Jerry would release Caroline, just the tips of their fingers touching, then he would draw her back in, and they would spin around, laughing inside, and skate on down the ice. Caroline seemed to be enjoying herself a lot. She was a good kid.

Jerry had been concentrating on Caroline so much that he was surprised when he looked away and saw that the whole gang was watching them waltz across the pond.

We're a big hit, he said, nodding to the onlookers.

When Caroline realized they had an audience, she self-consciously tried to stop, her blade catching a ridge on the ice. She lost her balance, and they fell in time, too.

The gang rushed over.

Are you guys all right?

I think so, said Jerry. *Caroline, are you hurt?*

I'm fine. Just a little bump.

We should probably sit and watch the others skate for awhile.

No, don't stop, the gang said. *You two were skating so beautifully.*

Yes, how long have you been skating together?

Well, actually this is our first date, Jerry explained.

You're kidding! Wow. Talk about a perfect match.

Caroline got a blushing expression on her face, although no blood filled her cheeks. It was pretty cold out there on the pond.

I think we'll catch our breaths, Jerry said, helping Caroline back up onto her feet.

They skated carefully over to the edge of the pond, stepping through the snowbank to a concrete bench. A weather-worn angel watched over them, a dollop of snow on her nose.

Jerry tried to call up the advice Bud had passed on to him. What did he say to talk about? A popular movie, friends they have in common, anything that is of mutual interest.

Movies were out. He hadn't seen one in ages. Friends? She was new in his neighborhood. Anything they were both interested in. That was the solution, but what did they share other than their place of residence? He didn't know.

Say something...

Uh, Caroline...

Yes, Jerry?

That's a lovely dress you're wearing.

Why, thank you. You look very nice, too.
Do I really? I mean, it's my only suit…
It looks fine.
And my skin. The flaking…the bugs…
She took both of his hands in hers. *Jerry, I like you. For yourself. I don't care about the bugs. Forget about the bugs. You'd have to be looking for them to see them. You have a good heart. I'm glad you asked me out. I'm having a fun time. I really am.*
Gosh, Caroline, you're really a neat person.
Silence, and then Jerry began to feel awkward. Think of something.
Then it struck him. How could I have missed it? The perfect topic for first date small talk. He knew Bud would be proud.
I like the smell of…dirt. Do you?
I didn't at first. But I think I'm getting used to it.
Me, too. I mean, I didn't like it at first either. But after awhile, it kind of, you know, gets under your skin.
Yes, I suppose it does.
In the springtime, they bring flowers.
I love flowers.
Sometimes, you can smell the rain.
I always liked rain. Rain makes the whole world fresh and new.
Sometimes, there are leaks.
I suppose so.
They chatted for awhile longer, swapping death stories—she and her folks expiring in a car wreck on an ice-coated highway, he succumbing to an inoperable brain tumor—then returned to the pond. The skating party broke up as the moon went down. Things were

going so well with Caroline that he didn't want to break the spell.

Caroline's mom and dad were inert when they got back. It was only a quarter to eleven.

I had a swell time tonight, said Caroline.

I'm glad you enjoyed the skating, Jerry said. *I'm glad you weren't hurt when you fell on the ice.*

I was more surprised than anything. All those people staring at us. It was like a dream.

They were having a good time together. But all good things, like life itself, must eventually come to an end.

Thank you for our date, Jerry said. *I had fun, too. I hope we can see each other again.*

So do I, Caroline said. *Please call for me anytime.*

In many communities, a good night kiss is expected as the customary way of ending a date. It can mean any number of things. A token of friendship, a simple way of saying thank you for the evening, a sign of affection. What it means depends on the two people and their definition of their relationship and themselves.

Jerry took the safe route. When Caroline rose, he squeezed her hand and searched for a smile.

The look on her face said she had a smile inside her, too.

And the date was over.

The next day, he told Bud about his evening with Caroline. Not in too much detail, because he didn't want to be one of those boys who doesn't respect a girl's privacy and reputation, and most importantly her personal feelings.

Your advice really helped me a lot, he told Bud.

Glad to be of service, guy.

I'm not sure what to do next. Should I wait a few days before calling her again? I don't feel like waiting. But I don't want her to think I'm too pushy either.

There's no perfect answer to your question. It depends on the two people and their definition of their relationship and themselves.

Gosh, I don't know, Bud. It all sounds pretty complicated.

It's the easiest thing in the world. You could call her today just to thank her for going with you to the skating party. That's a common courtesy. A girl would appreciate the gesture. Remember, though , to have a sensible attitude. Your call shouldn't go on for hours.

Should I ask her out again when I call?

After your courtesy call, I would wait a couple of days. By then it will be mid-week, and it will still give her several days notice. Remember, though, not to call her so late that she thinks she's the last resort.

So Jerry did call Caroline later that day, and handled it just the way Bud suggested. Although he yearned to talk to Caroline for hours, he kept it short. She seemed to genuinely appreciate his thoughtfulness.

Her receptive attitude toward him made his next call easy.

Hi Caroline, it's Jerry.

Hi, Jerry. How are you?

I'm doing very well, thank you. And yourself?

Just fine, thanks.

I was wondering, Caroline if you would like to go on a hayride this Saturday? The whole gang is going.

Oh, I'd love to, Jerry.

Great. I'll come for you around six, if that's okay.

That would be perfect. I'll see you then, Jerry.

Thank you, Caroline. Goodbye.

Jerry passed the week in a daze. A wonderful new world was opening up for him. He thought about Caroline constantly, and eagerly anticipated their next engagement. A hayride would be the ideal second date. You don't ask just anyone to go on a hayride. Skating is something you do separately, but a hayride is something you do…together. There could be several opportunities for floating his arm around her shoulder. Sweet. Bud strongly approved, too. Everything was going to be a shining golden sky.

And then disaster turned his social life on its ear.

Actually, more toward the front of his head.

One moment his left eyeball was tucked snugly into its socket where it belonged, the next moment it had migrated down his cheek, like a mouse peeking out of its hole.

The rotting must have progressed further than he realized. Jerry knew it was inevitable, although he hadn't cared to dwell on it, but why did it have to happen now? This week? So close to the hayride?

He tried to look on the bright side. The eye was still attached. That was worth something. Jerry tried to recall anatomy. Was it the optic nerve that secured the eyeball to the socket? And when that disintegrated…

What a fix.

Jerry immediately sought out Bud. He had to help. He just had to. Both of his eyes had long since vacated the premises. He must know what to do.

After hearing his dilemma, Bud said, *Well heck, I'd lend you mine, if I still had any.*

Can't we just pop it back in?

Afraid not. The normal rotting of tissue, plus the bugs, plus...

Okay, okay. So what am I going to do? I have a date with Caroline on Saturday. We're going on a hayride. I can't let her see me like this.

Don't call attention to it and she'll hardly notice.

How could she not notice? My eye is hanging halfway down my face for gosh sake.

Try to keep her on the side of your good eye.

I don't think that's going to solve much.

Listen, Jerry. This is just in the nature of things. You can't stop it. I can't stop it. We just do the best we can with what we have left of ourselves. Death goes on.

But Caroline...

You think she really likes you?

Yes. I do.

Then it won't matter. Consider this: if one of her eyes fell out of her head, would you stop seeing her?

Well, no...

There, you see? She probably feels exactly the same way.

But she's so pretty.

They're always pretty, in the beginning.

But what should I say to her?

Be straightforward. Girls appreciate that. There's no need to get graphic, of course. Avoid the temptation to seek sympathy. Have a positive, accepting attitude. You still have one good eye, don't you?

Well, yes...

If you let her know you're disturbed by it, then you'll just end up making her feel uncomfortable. She'll be glad to follow your lead. Once you explain the situation, don't bring it up again. Soon, you won't even remember that your eye is out of its socket, dangling there.

I don't know, Bud...

It will work, Jerry. Trust me. I haven't steered you wrong so far, have I?

Bud was right. His advice had been invaluable. He had common sense in bushels. Jerry didn't want to spring any surprises on Caroline, so on Saturday morning he called for her.

Hi, Caroline. This is Jerry.

Well hi, Jerry. How are you?

I'm fine, Caroline. And yourself?

Fine, thank you. We're still on for tonight, aren't we?

Yes, of course. But, uh, there's a little problem.

A problem?

I'm just having some trouble with my eye.

Nothing too serious, I hope.

Oh, no, no.... It's just, well, not exactly in the socket anymore. It's sort of... hanging down.

My goodness.

I mean, it's still attached. No doubt about that.

Yes, of course.

Silence.

I'm sorry, Jerry said.

It's okay. I understand, I really do.

You do?

I sure do. You still have one good eye, don't you?

Yes.

Well there you go.

You mean you don't mind, Caroline? You'll still go on the hayride with me?

Yes, I'll still go on the hayride with you, silly. You're still the same person I went skating with, aren't you?

Gosh, Caroline, you're really a swell girl.

So I'll see you this evening and I don't want to hear another word about it.

So long, Caroline. And thank you.

Jerry put the eye out of his mind.

A few minutes before six he came to Caroline. It's wise to leave a little early for a date. That way, there's no need to rush when you arrive at your date's residence. Makes for a more relaxed and enjoyable experience for everyone.

Hi, Jerry.

Hi, Caroline. Good evening, Mr. and Mrs. Ames.

He felt a warm greeting. Apparently he met with their approval.

Caroline looked beautiful. White dress, beads, peace, etc.

You look just like yourself, said Jerry.

Thank you, Jerry. That's sweet of you to say.

Are you all ready then? Jerry asked.

All set. 'Night mom and dad. We'll be back by ten-thirty.

Good night, Mr. and Mrs. Ames. Don't worry, I'll take good care of Caroline.

When they arrived at the hayride, the gang was already piling into the rotting hay wagon. Jerry had a few kernels of uneasiness as they approached the wagon. Someone was hooking a chestnut mare into its bridle. Large chunks of flesh were missing from the horse's flanks. Much of its head was eaten away, a part of the jawbone showing. Nobody was making a fuss about it. Jerry felt his self-confidence soar.

When they reached the business end of the wagon, Jerry stepped up first, and offered Caroline a hand. She took it and he pulled her up.

Hi gang, Jerry said.

Hi Jerry, the gang replied. *Nice to see you, Caroline.*

Hi everybody! Caroline said.

Jerry found a spot for them in the hay. He positioned himself so that Caroline had to sit on the side of his good eye. No sense drawing attention to the flaw if it could be easily avoided.

In a short time the driver hopped up on the front of the wagon, and gently shook the frayed reins. The skeletal horse broke into a trot, its sleigh bells sounding like a death rattle, the wagon rocking forward with the motion.

The driver guided the horse along the narrow trail that wound around the frozen pond and through the snowy field. Pines trees, statuary and ornate white buildings passed by.

What a wonderful idea this was, Caroline said. *This is really fun.*

I'm glad you came along.

Caroline patted Jerry on the forearm, then her fingers began to slide down toward his wrist, a clear sign that she was interested in holding hands.

Fortunately, Jerry first glanced down at her hand, then saw his own…

Immediately, he brought his arm across his chest and thrust his hand into the hay. Then, he reached across with his left hand and took hers.

I think I got a sliver, he explained.

Oh, let me see. I can take it out.

Well it's in pretty deep. I'll remove it later. It doesn't hurt much at all, really.

This seemed to satisfy her.

Her fingers were cold, and his were gone.

Not all of them, perhaps two, possibly three. All he saw were black, rotted stumps. The digits must have fallen off after he hoisted her up onto the wagon. He didn't even feel their departure. Were they in the wagon? He scanned the bed in the vicinity of where he had been standing, but he couldn't spot them amid the hay and snow. They must have fallen into the snow back on the trail. He'd never find them. And even if he did, what good would they do him now?

Caroline must not have noticed. Otherwise, she wouldn't have tried to hold that hand.

The rest of the hayride Jerry spent in nervous preoccupation with his missing appendages. The eye was bad enough. He didn't want Caroline to think he was coming apart on her.

Why now? Why all of a sudden? It was almost like the more he tried to have a social life, the more his body rebelled.

When the hay wagon returned to their point of departure, the horse collapsing into dust, Jerry helped Caroline down to the ground with his left hand, keeping his right tucked into the pocket of his best suit. He didn't dare search the vicinity for his fingers now.

The gang hung out afterwards, gossiping and cracking wise like dead teenagers do. Jerry struggled to keep in good spirits. When they got back to her place, it was later than he expected.

Dating Secrets of the Dead

Say, look at the time, said Jerry. *I told your folks I'd get you home by ten-thirty and here it is, almost eleven.*

I'm sure they'd understand. We aren't very late at all. There was nothing we could do about it, really.

I don't want your parents to think I'm taking advantage of you.

They won't think that. You can stay for awhile. I mean it.

Thank you for the offer, Caroline. I would just feel better if I took a rain check. You understand, don't you?

Oh, of course. You're such a gentleman, Jerry. Next time, I won't let you off the hook so easily.

Good night, Caroline.

Good night, Jerry. She leaned over and kissed him on the cheek, deftly avoiding his droopy eye. Her lips were still chilly from the hayride.

Jerry told Bud the bad news when he returned to his plot.

Fingers rotting away, eh? Join the club.

But what can I do about it? I can't keep company with Caroline like this. She was okay with my eye, but I can't expect her to pretend forever. How are we supposed to hold hands?

Do it spiritually. Girls like a boy who has a kind heart. It makes them feel special.

I want to feel Caroline, touch her.

Use your other hand.

I did, but how long will that last? I'm surprised it's still attached.

There's no turning back, Jerry. There's an old saying around here: If you don't rest in peace, you'll come apart in pieces.

David Prill

Look, my prospects aren't too good anyway. I appreciate your willingness to help me, Bud. I'll think of something. Maybe if we can keep going on group dates I can hide it from her.

And then what?

I don't know. I don't know. I'll come up with something.

Jerry knew he had to apologize to Caroline, after his behavior on the hayride.

The next day he called for her, trying to inject sunshine into his voice. He remembered sunshine, wistfully.

Hi Caroline, this is Jerry.

Hello, Jerry. How are you?

Very well, thanks.

That's good. I had a really fun time on the hayride, Jerry. Thank you for taking me.

I enjoyed it, too. That's why I was calling, Caroline. I wanted to apologize for my behavior at your place. I shouldn't have run off like that. You said it was okay if I hung around, and I should have trusted you.

Oh, gosh Jerry, there's no need to apologize. I understand. You were just trying to be sweet.

You're not mad at me then?

Of course not.

Wow, that's great to hear, Caroline. I wasn't sure. I mean, I didn't know. My eye...

You're fine, Jerry.

How about if I make it up to you anyway? The gang is going sledding this afternoon. Do you want to go?

Well, to be honest, Jerry, I was hoping we could do something by ourselves once.

Oh no...

Uh, what did you have in mind?

24

Why don't we just go for a walk? What do you say?

Jerry knew what he had to say.

Sure, Caroline, that sounds swell. What time do you want me to come over?

How about three?

Three it is.

Terrific. I'll see you then.

Goodbye, Caroline.

Jerry spent the rest of the day wringing his hand.

He couldn't keep his problem in his pocket all afternoon. He had to be honest with Caroline. If only they had given me gloves, he thought with high melancholy.

Three o' clock came like it couldn't wait to see him humiliated.

Jerry hated the fact that he felt trepidation about seeing Caroline. He wanted to feel excitement, anticipation, affection. Not this squeamish, nervous feeling.

On the way over to Caroline's, Jerry felt an odd sensation and it had nothing to do with his interior life. Something in the region of his feet. Suddenly he had trouble walking. And he didn't have to look to know that his toes had been eaten away by time or worms or some burrowing creature.

Jerry didn't get upset, just philosophical. He had hit some kind of plateau, gone from a being with one foot in this world and the other foot in the next, to both feet on the verge of rotting off his legs.

When his deterioration had been easy to hide, it had been possible to keep up appearances, pass as something he was not.

But now, with a dangling eye, stumps instead of fingers, a lot of extra space down at the end of his polished black shoes, there was only one path to take.

Jerry presented himself to Caroline as he was, a young man on the downside of his death.

He hobbled the rest of the way to her place.

She was waiting for him, smelling the plastic flowers. An ice-crusted bouquet of pale purples, reds and yellows.

Hi, Caroline.

Oh hi, Jerry. I didn't hear you coming. She looked at him with concern. *Are you okay? You're walking so strangely.*

This was it.

Well, Caroline, you see, my feet are rotting away. And my hand. He displayed it for her. And tried to force a smile on his natural and peaceful face. *I'm a real mess, aren't I?*

Maybe we should just stay here today. We could talk or something.

I want to walk, said Jerry. *Please walk with me, Caroline.*

Sure, Jerry. I'll walk with you.

They slowly strolled among the monuments and trees, stark oaks coated with ice, evergreens hanging heavy with snow. The moon was circled by a pale orange halo.

Why is it happening now, so fast? Caroline gently asked him. *Just the other day you were fine.*

Bud says it's because I won't rest in peace.

Have I met Bud?

I'm not sure. Bud Pollard. 1959-1976. Loving son devoted student friend of the community.

Oh, yes, I remember seeing him.

He's a good guy. He's always given me helpful advice.

I'm so sorry, Jerry. What are you going to do?

They had reached a bench sheltered by a hedge planted in an arc. With every step it seemed harder for Jerry to walk properly. His gait was a rolling, teetering travesty.

Let's sit down, Jerry said, and she helped him do that.

She was seated on his left, so he was able to hold her hand properly.

Caroline put her head on his shoulder. The decay hadn't hit there yet.

We need to have a talk, Jerry said.

Okay.

They looked at each other, his dangling eye trying to get into the act, too.

You know, Caroline, you're the first girl I've kept company with since I came here. And even if I would have known that dating you would make me decompose to beat the band, I wouldn't have changed a thing, that's how much I've treasured our time together.

I feel the same way. Listen, Jerry, pretty soon what's happening to you will overtake me, too. My eyeballs will go pop, toes and fingers fall off, bits and pieces eaten away. And the bugs...

We have this time together. We have the present, before all that happens.

Yes, isn't it wonderful?

Yes, but I'm withering away so quickly, said Jerry. *I don't know how long I've got before I won't be able to go for walks, or ice skating, or anything.*

Your suit still looks sharp.

27

David Prill

I don't want to rush us, Caroline, but those are the facts. If we let the days go by thinking things will always be the way they are now, one day we'll wake up and I'll just be a pile of sludge you used to call a friend.

Oh, Jerry, please, don't talk like that.

We have to face it, Caroline. We can't deny this. He reached out for her with his rotting stump. She drew her hand away.

He gazed grimly at her. *This is our future, Caroline. In a few days you're going to be afraid to even look at me.*

A few remnant tears squeezed themselves from her barren ducts. *I won't be afraid, Jerry. I promise.*

Jerry hesitated for a moment. *What I'm saying, Caroline, is that if you want us to have any sort of...physical relationship, we can't wait.*

Caroline's peaceful, natural face was clouded with sadness.

I'm sorry it has to be like this, said Jerry. *I know this isn't considered good dating etiquette. It's not proper to pressure a girl into intimate relations. If there was another way...*

No, you're right, she said. *We have to face this. I don't want death to be denial, too.*

They sat in quiet spaces for a time, holding hands. A nuthatch lit on an evergreen branch, then flew off when it realized it wasn't alone. Its weight disturbed the branch, sending a dusting of snow down upon the heads of the dead.

So, Caroline, Jerry said shyly, *do you want to go back to my place?*

•

Jerry's place was in bad need of a dusting.

It's not much, he said, *but it's home.*

I like it. It's cozy.

Are you comfortable? he asked her.

I'm just fine. It's nice to be so close to you.

Don't worry about hurting me.

I won't. Can we do something about that eye? It's sort of in the way.

Oh, sure. Hang on...got it. Is that better?

Much better. Now I can touch your face, all over.

He began to touch her, too.

You don't think I'm easy, Jerry, do you?

No, of course not.

Have there been other girls...like me?

No, only the living.

That makes me feel good.

As they began to probe and pet, and then proceed to the most private of realms, Jerry began to feel parts of himself break away, disintegrate. His fine suit slowly collapsed in upon itself, soaking up what remained of his bodily fluids.

Jerry suddenly felt disgusted, even horrified and he didn't know why.

I have very strong feelings for you, Caroline whispered to him.

I feel the same about you.

What's wrong with me? he wondered. This should be the crowning moment of my death. Why do I feel so terrible, so guilt-wracked, so...wrong?

Caroline sensed it, too. *What's going on? Are you okay?*

I'm okay, he said. *I'm okay.*

But he wasn't. This felt so wrong, so...immoral.

David Prill

At the very moment they consummated their deaths, as his body rotted away to utter uselessness, a shock of awareness hit him, as he understood what had disturbed him, why everything had felt so wrong.

And why now everything was feeling so right.

The final dating secret.

Jerry realized, as both of Caroline's eyes popped out upon her climax, and their precious ooze commingled, that if a living person has intimate relations with a dead body, it's called necrophilia.

If two dead bodies have intimate relations, it must be love.

CARNYVORE

We Invite the Guests

Our death began in Elmville, Minnesota.

The freaks were the first to get the axe. Rikki, the Dog-Faced Mind Reader. Ben, the Human Dartboard. Medusa Maggie. Five-Footed Frank. All of them. The whole Cavalcade of Human Oddities.

Due to the potential for emotional damage to our children, and the negative impact on public safety, dehumanizing displays of human deformities will no longer be permitted within the city limits of Elmville. Any carnival or other traveling show that attempts to present such displays will be subject to fines and a permanent revocation of the required city permits. Sincerely, Lewis Randle, Police Chief, Elmville.

Minnesota always had the reputation in the carnival business as a great freak show state. Although inbreeding was generally frowned upon, there was a certain sameness to the blonde-haired, emotionally reserved natives, so anything even mildly off-trail seemed mind-bendingly bizarre to them.

The edict spread like the clap from town to town throughout the Upper Midwestern circuit.

Like any other hurtful gossip.

Like any other lie.

Our freaks weren't hurting no one. They were in our show because nobody else wanted them. What were you so scared of, Mr. Police Chief?

It was like losing a limb.

But we carried on. The show must go on. Not for any idealistic, head-in-the-big-top notions. Because of our crying stomachs and dry throats and the need to keep a flimsy trailer roof over our heads.

The good-bye party for the freaks lasted two drunken days, in some dusty field in the nothing that is southwestern Minnesota. It would have lasted longer, but the bonfire caught the attention of the cops. Guns drawn, faces white and wide-eyed, until we explained what bad dreams of theirs we were. They were nice about kicking us out of the county, at least.

The last image we remember, the image we will carry with us forever, is the faces of the freaks in the dirty rear window of the camper van, hands if they had them flat against the windows, eyes if they had them sad and lost. And tears. Whatever else they were, whatever body part was distorted by nature, they all had tears. Then the night closed over them and they were gone.

Later we heard that the freaks had tried to settle down in a residential neighborhood outside of St. Paul. A full week before the first firebomb. This came after the obscene phone calls and rock throwing. Five-Footed Frank got first-degree burns on four of the five and died of an infection soon after. Freaks had endured the torment from normals since the beginning of time, it came with their twisted territory — the insults, the stares, fellow humans crossing the street rather than crossing their path. Their own deformities were nothing compared to this burden.

So they moved out and tried again, this time in a trailer park on the outskirts of the Cities. Same result, as if firebombs were as common as barbecues in these bottom-feeding neighborhoods. No casualties this time. A fluke.

Finally the freaks surrendered and moved up to a hobby farm near Duluth. Here they found some solace, among God's creatures, hearts rising at the occasional discovery of a two-headed calf or three-legged frog. Exiled from the rest of society, but at least they had each other. Freak Farm, the locals called it. Eventually they began to grow organic vegetables, which they sold from a stand along the highway. They earned a form of respect from their neighbors, and were able to live in a quarantined peace.

The rest of Wiltern Brothers' Carnival and Big Top Extravaganza carried on. We would survive the loss of the freaks. Receipts from the freak shows had been declining in recent years anyway, the Wiltern Brothers, midgets themselves, assured us. Nothing would change.

It seemed like they were right. Our first post-freak show, in Swaydall, Minnesota, felt tighter, more focused. The customers, packed more closely together down the pathways of the carnival, gave our mournful troupe a needed shot of juice. And the more energetic, upbeat, and happy the patrons feel, the easier it is to pry the folded money from their wallets.

Some of the older patrons missed the freaks, almost like distant relatives who came through town once a year, and said so and didn't care who heard them. The bulk of the ticket buyers, however, were used to taking whatever was given them without a complaint or comment or even a turn of the head. That's the way they had been trained.

Vagabonds like us were immune to this sort of social hypnotism. We lived on the road, made our beds in dirty, sunstroke-inducing vacant lots. Even the trailer trash looked down on us. We were trained in what we knew, the carnival, and knew nothing more.

●

The hillside is dark. The city lights wink off early, long before any of us are even tired.

●

We Prepare the Meal

The next to fall were the games of chance. The Plush Wheel, the Cat Pitch, the Cane Rack, the Birthday Joint. Every last one.

Gambling is a disease. It tempts God-loving people to waste money they should be using to buy children clothes and food and toys. The gambler spends his time at the gambling table instead of at the dinner table, with his family. Gambling destroys families and corrupts the moral fiber of our town. Any enterprise that promotes gambling is not wel-

come in our town. Yours in the Lord, Pastor Hal Merriwether, Loving Lamb Lutheran Church, Elmville.

Of course, it was never much of a gamble for us. In the Cat Pitch, for example, the patron has three chances to tip over three of the dozens of fluffy kitties standing shoulder to shoulder at the back of the store. Easy, right? The solid bodies on those cats comprise less than a third of their total apparent width, most of which is light fluff standing straight out from the sides. A hurled baseball can pass through that airy fluff without so much as disturbing the cats' whiskers.

So from the pulpit to the city council room to our show the message was sent, and the games, and the operators, had to go. They weren't cartoon characters or a punch line from a tasteless joke; they were real people, with hopes and dreams and families and friends.

The Wiltern Brothers found work within the show for a few of the operators, but the rest were sent packing. We heard some of them caught on with other shows, and the rest just disappeared into the cornfed Midwestern horizon. Where's the morality in that, Mr. Pastor Merriwether?

•

The streets in town are empty, except for us. We creep through the shadows, hoping the town is sleeping tight.

•

David Prill

We Set the Table

The animals were next up on the chopping block. From Jezebel the Elephant to Bob the Pony to even the star of the Mouse Run.

It's amazing that in the twenty-first century animals are still being exploited for profit in such a horrific manner. This is one step up from cockfighting. The animals are mistreated and abused and subject to humiliating themselves for our supposed amusement. There's nothing amusing about an elephant tethered to a post in the hot sun all day or a tiger confined in a filthy cage. Animals should be free to live their lives like any other creature on this planet. Any show that mistreats animals should not be granted a license in our town. Respectfully, Audrey Winstead, Director, Elmville County Humane Society.

This one was a shocker. In the city, it would have made sense. City folk are cut off from the life-and-death realities of the world. They think milk comes out of a bottle and meat magically appears in the cold case at Red Owl. But in a small town, with so many farms in the vicinity, and so many hunters...I think the animal rights fanatics were jumping on the anti-carnival bandwagon, which by then was starting to look more like a hearse. We were an easy target, and with no local ties, nobody was going to bother sticking up for us. The hunters and farmers probably figured if they let the animal rights predators have us, they'd leave normal good gun-toting citizens alone.

Look, Freddy the Mouse wasn't being exploited. He had a nice life, no worse than any of us. We all had jobs to do. In the Mouse Run, the bowl is placed over Freddy, bets are placed, and whoever picks which of the three holes on the perimeter of the table Freddy runs into is the winner. A little vinegar placed just inside one of the holes can influence Freddy's decision, but he was always unpredictable. He did his routine for a few hours every night, and then the rest of the time he spent snoozing in his big cage, or eating, or playing on the wheel. Not a bad life.

In little towns far from the city, the carnival is for many children their first chance to see exotic animals. TV isn't a substitute. TV is not real. We are real. We're an educational show.

Children love us. Children have always loved us. Children understand.

But from one town to the next the blind decree passed. The animals had to go, if we were to survive. So Jezebel and Bob and all the rest were sold back to our regular dealer, and where they ended up after that is anybody's guess.

Freddy the Mouse was donated to a grade school. For the children.

•

The clowns lead the way. Not for any theatrical reason, but because our clowns have some experience with breaking and entering. Every con deserves a second chance. In small towns, they have finally begun locking their doors at night, but the windows are seldom secured, and the screens can be cut like paper.

•

David Prill

We Say Grace

The noose was tightening around our necks. They were stripping away our cotton-candy facade and getting right down to our core, our heart, and we wondered if they would like what they saw when we were laid bare.

Don't worry, said the Wiltern Brothers, we still have our cash cow. We still have our rides.

The rides.

Wipeout.

Roll-O-Plane.

Gravitron.

Scrambler.

Octopus.

Bumble Bees.

Go-Gator.

Phantom Phyler.

Tubs of Fun.

Quadzilla.

We still had our rides.

Until the accidents.

One sweltering Saturday evening in New Ulm a coupling on the Scrambler disengaged, sending a pair of cars hurtling into the night. The operator, Manny Jenks, managed to shut down the ride before any of the other cars went sailing. We were lucky there. A couple of broken bones, a concussion or two, gashes and bruises. Nothing fatal.

The Gravitron was another story. This incident coincidentally took place in Madelia, a mere five miles down the highway from everyone's favorite hamlet, Elmville. A visitor happened to have a video camera rolling — his grandson was inside. He caught the whole disaster, in shaky screaming dying color. The footage even made it onto cable news, and eventually was picked up by God knows how many local stations grateful for a shocking video clip to keep viewers tuned in during the summer doldrums.

The Gravitron, if you haven't had the pleasure of climbing aboard, is a purple flying saucer. The patrons lay along the walls, hanging onto the hand holds. The disc begins to spin, slowly at first and when it reaches a certain speed it begins to rotate on its axis, producing a feeling of weightlessness in the riders. It's the most popular ride in the show, so we set it up at the very end of the Midway, to force the patrons to warm up their terror with some of the other rides along the way. The Gravitron is always jammed with kids on weekend nights.

Well, on the weekend night in question, something went terribly not quite right. The saucer somehow slipped off its spindle and in a shower of sparks went careening down the hillside behind the Midway, finally slamming into a stand of poplar trees ringing a muddy pond. Good thing the trees were there, otherwise the body count would have been far higher than three.

Wasn't our fault. Our safety record had always been excellent. Look, it was in our own interest to keep the rides in top-notch shape. A single accident in a season can mean the difference between a tolerable full-bodied case of beer and that watered-down 3.2 swill.

At every stop there is supposed to be a local inspector who examines the rides before the gates open. This time the regular inspector, a retiree who used to be a mechanic for the railroad, was out of town. His replacement was a kid who had zero experience in the field. The kid didn't know what to look for, and couldn't have spotted a problem if it had him by the neck and was choking the guts out of him.

We probably would have caught the broken linchpins ourselves, but some of the operators who had been laid off in earlier waves of persecution also doubled up in our ride maintenance department.

We became a scapegoat again.

Carnival rides are inherently unsafe. These fly-by-night operators roll into town and are only interested in taking our money. They have no interest in protecting our children, and so tragedy inevitably is the sad result. Since there is no way to adequately ensure that these rides have undergone any type of thorough maintenance and inspection program before they enter our city limits, we have no choice but to ban all Midway-style rides from our town. These rides include but are not limited to Wipeout, Roll-O-Plane, Gravitron, Scrambler, Octopus, Bumble Bees, Go-Gator, Phantom Phyler, Tubs of Fun, Quadzilla, blah blah blah. Your humble servant, Dr. Fenton Briggs, Mayor of Elmville.

•

The list was complete, and so from house to house we go, taking our victims from their beds with the skill of a pickpocket. When we have gathered all the participants, we head back through the darkness to the even darker tents.

Hurry hurry hurry.
The show is about to begin.

•

We Eat the Meal

See, they stripped away everything from our show.
Our Freaks.
Our Games of Chance.
Our Exotic Animals.
Our Rides.
Our Wiltern Brothers, who were like fathers to us. They died of broken hearts after receiving the fateful letter from the mayor.
They took it all.
Except for one thing.
The essence of the show.
Its true heart.
Us.
The Carnies.
We are the true Freaks.
We are a twisted prize on the Wheel of Fortune.
We are the rabid, fully clawed animals.
We are the deep and dark Midway ride that never ends.
Everything you ever heard about us is true. Every rumor, every fear, every campfire story, every nightmare, all true.
There's something else that's true, too.
The show must go on.

The audience is waiting, on the edge of their seats. Well, on the edge anyway. They just showed up, all the area's misfits and unwanted. Mostly kids. Mostly those who ran afoul of authority figures all their lives. They're all wearing magic smiles. They have no clue what they're about to see. They must be clueing in on the special looks on our faces.

So we've got the four of them, hands cuffed behind their backs, soiled canvas sacks tied tight over their heads. We herd them through the ramshackle illicit carnival grounds into the dark tent, under the Big Bad Top. They are saying things, frantic, urgent things, but we can't understand them because the canvas is muffling their voices, see. We've heard enough of what they've had to say already.

One by one we remove the hoods. One by one their red and terrified heaving faces are revealed. It's like Christmas morning for us, a trip to Hell for them. It's nice to be happy for a change.

One by one.

Lewis Randle, Police Chief.

Pastor Hal Merriwether, Loving Lamb Lutheran Church.

Audrey Winstead, Director, Elmville County Humane Society.

Dr. Fenton Briggs, Mayor.

And then our New Carnival begins.

•

The Police Chief, the freak killer, is first. Only he doesn't look so much like a Police Chief anymore. He looks more like Grotesquely Twisted Limbs Chief or Ten-Penny Nails in the Head Chief. He sits in a small tent in the dark Midway and looks blankly as visitors come in, gawk at him, make smart-ass comments, and then with their makeshift tools, accelerate his entry into the Kingdom of the Deformed.

●

The Pastor is next on the hit parade. This game of chance has a little higher stakes than the church's bingo games the Pastor has so conveniently overlooked in his diatribe against us.

Now he is a game of chance incarnate. He is pinned spread-eagled on a board with a variety of colorful balloons attached to his torso. The counter at the booth is packed with darts, red, green and blue, the patrons snatching handfuls of them and not doing a very good job of winning prizes. They are aiming too high. The Pastor's face is beginning to look a lot like Christmas. A candycane. A Santa suit. Lots of red on a pale white face. Eye shots are met with hoots and cheers, which inspire the throwers' aim even more.

We wonder what the chances are of the Pastor coming out of this night with his collar and the rest of his body intact. Probably not good. It's a popular booth, as many of our visitors have apparently experienced his disapproval.

Step right up, folks.

Everybody's a winner.

Except for the Pastor, of course.

Say your prayers, pal.

David Prill

●

Audrey the Humane Society Director is a problem. There are calls from the audience to spare her.

You can see the hope in her sweaty squeamish face.

However, once we explain the situation, how we're an educational show, and that in little towns far from the city the carnival is for many children their first chance to see exotic animals real and live and not on the TV, and that Audrey had single-handedly stolen the magic animal childhood memory from the youngsters, the audience understands, and the calls resume, although to be frank the calls for sparing her, if any, are drowned out by the calls to do other things to her.

There are good suggestions from the audience, but we already have something special in mind for the head of the Humane Society. And the rest of her, too.

We call it the Audrey Run.

In the Audrey Run the burn barrel is placed over Audrey, bets are placed, and whoever picks which of the three sinkholes on the perimeter of the woods Audrey falls into is the winner. Two of the sinkholes are dry, one is filled with murky water. It's deep. We spin her around so she can't get her bearing. A swath of oil placed just outside one of the holes can influence Audrey's decision, but she's always unpredictable.

It's not as easy to drown someone as you might think.

But it's not *that* hard either.

●

44

Your turn, Mr. Mayor, Mr. Dr. Fenton Briggs.

We saved the worst for last, you Executioner of Rides. You brought the Gravitron back to earth. You rubbed out the Tubs of Fun. You made the Go-Gator into a pair of alligator shoes. You plucked off the arms of the Octopus, tentacle by tentacle, slowly, methodically, cruelly.

You knew your actions would result in the death of the Wiltern Brothers Carnival. You knew it. You could have reformed the regulations and let us live. That would have been the decent thing to do.

But you smelled blood.

And you killed us dead, like spraying a can of insecticide on the Bumble Bees.

We have a problem, though, Mr. Dr. Mayor Fenton Briggs.

We have an audience of not-so-nice folks who came to our carnival expecting there would be rides. Scary rides, rides that would cause their hearts to blast up into their throats and their innards to roil.

But we have no rides that are legal in the City of Elmville.

So we have to create a new ride.

And you can help.

The line is long, as one by one the audience climbs aboard the hooded handcuffed shrieking Mayor, driving him into the dirt, reaming him utterly.

•

David Prill

We Clear the Table

It was a quality show. We congratulate ourselves on making lemons out of lemonade, good old-fashioned family entertainment out of the blood of our enemies.

Members of the audience mob us after the show and express their admiration. Some want to run away and join our after-hours carnival.

We don't know what to say.

We are…*flattered!*

This night was supposed to be a one-shot orgy of revenge, a night not only to wreak hell on those who drove the Wiltern Brothers out of business, but a broader statement against all those sideways glances, snide remarks, and general shit that we and all of our brothers and sisters have been forced to endure from the likes of you over the years. And during the frenzy it did seem like higher powers were inside us, spurring us on, inspiring us, as if we were connected to all Carnies living and dead and everywhere in between.

When our stomachs are full, we leave the carnage to the crows and don't bother to clean ourselves, never again to clean ourselves, never again to make even a nod toward respectability.

And while we are busy not cleaning ourselves, we are…*thinking.*

And believe me, our thoughts aren't very respectable either.

•

We Say Goodnight

Elmville is nothing special.

There are many, many Elmvilles in Minnesota and throughout the Upper Midwest. You can't swing a dead mayor without hitting one.

There was nothing special about Police Chief Randle, or Pastor Merriwether, or Humane Society Director Audrey, or Mayor Briggs either.

The cast of characters is always the same, no matter where the night takes you. Only the minor details change. Hair color, body type, first name, last name, the pitch of their screams. Whatever. Their hearts are identical, and that's what counts.

Every town has its collection of lovely misfits, too. People like us.

Call it a carnyval. A carnevil. A carnageval.

Whatever it is, it's bad news for the likes of you.

Coming soon and without fanfare to your town some chilly fall night. You are unable to sleep and you get up and look out the window, and along with the dead leaves blowing down the boulevard you see a group of dark figures, hunched over, coming down the street in the wake of the leaves. You think you see clowns leading the way, dirty-looking clowns with deranged smiles and cutting tools. Must be dreaming, you think.

Keep that thought. Go back to bed.

Unless your standing is high in the community. Unless you have a habit of making phony moral pronouncements that keep people like us down. Then you had better seek higher ground. Then you had better run.

David Prill

Unless you are an outsider. Unless you have felt their contempt, been humiliated by their disdain. If you're out there, then come out here, into the darkened streets of the cesspool called your hometown.

Join us.

Come see the show.

We are hungry.

We haven't eaten in days.

Set yourself a place at the table.

And *eat.*

Television and the VCR put show business out of business. There ain't none left. A guy gets off from work, he goes by the 7-Eleven, he gets a case of beer, two bottles of wine, three bags of chips, two chip dips, he goes home and gets in a recliner and you couldn't get him out with a double-barrel shotgun. Now that's a helluva way to live, isn't it?

— former spook show operator Jim Ridenour

THE LAST HORROR SHOW

Death on the Slab

How did Dr. Morbid die?

Was his head severed from his neck by a buzz saw? Was he thrown off the stage, one piece at a time? Did he get fourteen knives through the head, death on the slab, the final blackout?

Hollywood starlet Ronni Dukes called with the news. I hadn't heard from her in years, although I often dreamed of her. I wondered if she was still doing the Twist.

It was over.

The end of the hyp bits, the hot seat, the snake throw, the ghosts who sit beside you and plant wet kisses on your cheek, the slave maidens at the mercy of hideous beasts, free hair dye for those whose hair turns white.

I loved the Doc. He made Frankenstein look like a sissy. Nowadays the world makes the Doc look like a sissy, and monsters walk among us.

The Doc's death didn't make the news. He wasn't news since the seventies and even then he fought for every scrap of attention, window card by window card, faint check by faint check.

It wasn't always this way.

Back in the 1960s, in the picnic of innocence called the Upper Midwest, long before the boy in me would leave for good, I witnessed the midnight spook shows ride the night like gaudy phantasms into the small towns and fresh-faced suburbs of my home state of Minnesota.

Here was another world, a lost world, a smorgasbord of insanity, every thrill in the book, a world so terrifying that only screams can describe it, free candles for those afraid to go home in the dark.

A world governed by a congress of madmen.

Dr. Evil and the Terrors of the Unknown.

Kara-Kum and the Crawling Thing from Planet #13.

Dr. Dracula's Living Nightmares.

Dr. Satan's Shrieks in the Night.

And most all, for me, Dr. Ogre Banshee and his Chasm of Spasms. Because that is where it all began.

1966
The Chasm of Spasms

My bike was my most important possession in the fall of 1966. A green Huffy 3-speed, with banana seat, ape-hanger handlebars, and miles of chrome. I had gotten it for my birthday the previous spring, and my life hadn't been the same since. It replaced a clunky red Huffy straight from the pages of the 1961 Sears Roebuck Wish Book. The older bike mirrored the cars of the time, boxy and maneuverable as a pontoon boat, and if they put fins on bikes, it probably would've had them too. I did swap the standard black tailbone-torturing seat with a leopard print banana seat, but it still had just one speed and I still had to brake with the pedals.

My new bike was a ticket to freedom. It was lightweight and fast and responded to my every move. No obstacles could slow us down. Asphalt and dirt, gravel and grass, fields and hills, creeks and mud holes, it didn't matter. We could fly anywhere.

In early October, I stayed on my bike constantly, trying to stretch out the fading cool nights as much as possible. It seemed like the sky got dark as soon as dinner was over.

I rode. There was nothing like the sound of the bike zipping through windswept piles of yellow and rusty red leaves. I was regretting the passing of summer, still not really caught up yet in the school year, knowing that soon I'd have to put the bike up into the garage rafters for the winter.

Halloween was close enough at hand to take seriously, and I was still young enough to take it very seriously. I was plotting a way I could ride my bike to gather treats this Halloween. I knew my folks wouldn't go for having me out riding after dark, in a bulky costume and a mask with dime-sized eyeholes. But the idea of hitting a hundred houses in one night gave me insomnia.

On Halloween I usually visited every occupied building within a half mile of my house, with two exceptions: apartment buildings and stores. I always skipped apartment buildings, because I was afraid. I don't think I had ever been in an apartment building in my life up to that point. I pictured men with loosened ties and five o'clock shadows, pouring hard liquor into glasses stacked with ice. And while I knew for a fact that some neighborhood stores like the Country Boy dairy store down the street also handed out candy, you had to go inside, come under the white tell-all glare of flourescent lights from the protecting darkness. You were no longer a creature of the night, just a kid in a cheap costume from Kresge's.

Any other day of the year, Country Boy was a mecca—it was my main source of baseball cards and comic books and Mouth Full bubble gum. So one muddy-sky October afternoon when my mom asked me to get her a carton of milk, and slipped me a quarter more than required, I didn't hesitate. Before the coins were cool in my pocket I was already trying to decide between the Justice League and the Flash.

I never made it to the dairy store.

I rode my bike up to the store, which was next door to Bob's North Star gas station.

As I climbed off my bike I noticed, on the edge of my vision, an unnatural vehicle parked at one of the white pumps. A real head-turner.

I had seen hearses before, usually at the front end of a procession of cars with headlights on, and a police escort. But an unescorted hearse, in my very own neighborhood...

Bob was busy wiping its blackened windows with a rag, acting like he was working on my folks' Ford Galaxie.

I forgot about the milk and pedaled warily over to the gas station.

I stopped. Something funny about this hearse.

Maybe it was the dead bloody body hanging out of the back, legs akimbo.

I couldn't believe what I was seeing. What had happened here? Did the hearse hit a bump on the way to the cemetery, propelling the body out the back door? Wouldn't Bob have noticed and said something? Maybe he hadn't noticed. Maybe nobody had noticed.

Slowly, I wheeled my bike toward the hearse. Bob was finished with the windshield and had headed back into his shop.

I stopped six feet from the rear of the hearse, leaning out over the handlebars, unable to take my eyes from the dead body, inching closer. The body looked very...stiff. The blood was the color of barn paint.

"Go ahead and touch him, kid."

I jumped back, nearly losing my balance.

A laugh. From a young thin man in a rumpled dark suit. He had appeared while I was engrossed with the corpse. He had a friendly look on his face, and didn't

55

look much older than the high school kids who hung out at the A&W parking lot devouring Teenburgers and picking up girls. His blonde hair was slicked back and he spoke with an easygoing Southern drawl. My eyes skipped from the dead body to the live man and back again. I wanted to touch the body. I wanted get home as fast as I could. I should have picked up the milk and kept my eyes from straying. Now it was too late.

"For real?"

"You're not scared?"

"I...no, I'm not scared."

The man approached me, closer, crouching down so that we were eye-to-eye. "Will you be scared when Southtown Theater becomes a graveyard, and the seats become coffins? When the ghosts, ghouls and zombies run wild? When the monsters grab girls from the audience and the living dead sit next to you? When you see people from the audience sawed in half and burned alive?" Now he was close enough that I could smell the liquor on his breath. "Do you think you'll be scared then?"

I gulped and couldn't speak. I got off my bike, carefully nudged down the kickstand. Heart thudding, sweating everywhere else, I stepped toward the dead body. I reached out to his lower leg, right below the blood stains.

I touched him.

Felt the scratchy material of his pants, embraced the leg with my small hand.

"It's not real," I said quietly, looking at the man wonderingly. "It's a fake."

He walked around to the passenger side of the hearse, and beckoned me over with a long finger. I followed him.

He nodded at the side panels of the hearse, which were plastered with red, yellow and orange posters.

SEE DR. OGRE BANSHEE AND HIS CHASM OF SPASMS!

GHOSTS, GHOULS AND ZOMBIES WILL RUN WILD!

MONSTERS GRAB GIRLS FROM THE AUDIENCE!

THE LIVING DEAD SIT NEXT TO YOU!

SEE PEOPLE FROM THE AUDIENCE SAWED IN HALF AND BURNED ALIVE!

I looked at the man again.

"You ever seen a spook show, partner?"

"No, sir."

"Would you like a free pass to the show?" He reached into his coat pocket and withdrew an orange ticket, just far enough so that I could see the face of a leering zombie which had been imprinted onto its surface. He must have seen the longing in my eyes, because he didn't bother waiting for me to reply before continuing. "Make you a deal," he said, casually, as if it wasn't the first time. "I need someone to be a ghost on the day of the show. Think you can handle it?"

"A ghost?"

"Yeah. You'll wear a sheet and parade around outside the theater, handing out flyers to people promoting the show. Are you interested?"

"For a free pass? Gosh, yes."

"It's a midnight show. Will your folks let you stay up that late?"

"I think so. I hope so. I'll ask them. They have to!"

"Great. Maybe you'll get lucky and win a real dead body to take home with you." He tucked the orange ticket back into his coat pocket.

"You're teasing me. I bet it's a fake, too."

His face grew grave. "We're giving away a real dead body, that's the honest truth I swear on a stack of skeletons."

"He really chops the heads off people?"

"Dr. Banshee has already chopped off the heads of approximately a dozen comely teenagers this week alone. But don't worry, he sharpens his saw blade every morning, so if he chooses your head you won't have to worry about him making a mess out of you."

I fingered my neck. "I don't want my head chopped off."

"I'll try to put in a good word for you with the Doc."

The man wasn't laughing. "Do you still want to do the ghost bit?"

I nodded with equal somberness.

"Then just be at the rear of the theater at twelve noon on the day of the show. We'll get you all set up and show you the ropes. What's your name?"

"David."

"Okay, Dave. My name's Don. You look like a good kid and I know you'll do a swell job. We're counting on you, all right?"

"I won't let you down. I promise."

As the hearse drove away, the dead body still dangling out the back end, the carton of milk and even

Halloween were completely forgotten. I couldn't believe it. Dr. Ogre Banshee and his Chasm of Spasms were coming to my town.

No matter whose head Dr. Banshee decided to chop off, I knew I had to be there.

•

Beginning the day after I encountered the dead body at Bob's North Star, the ballyhoo began. The town had transformed overnight. Posters appeared on telephone poles, light poles, fence posts, any bare surface was fair game for the Chasm of Spasms. Small placards suddenly appeared in Town Drug, Red Barn, Dave's Shoe Repair — everywhere I turned the lurid fantastic images and insane slogans confronted me.

All the dark and blood-soaked roads were leading to the Southtown Theater.

Southtown was the heart of our town. Santa Claus lived in a quaint cottage in the middle of the parking lot the month before Christmas. Casey Jones and Roundhouse Rodney, stars of *Lunch with Casey* and *Grandma Lumpett's Boarding House,* once performed in the parking lot and drew so many kids that I had to watch their antics on a television in a department store. Kresge's dime store was there, home of most of my toy soldiers. I got haircuts at Roy's Barber Shop, and long ago before I started school ate ham sandwiches at the Southtown Lanes while my mom bowled in her morning league. My second-grade class toured the meat locker at the Red Owl supermarket.

And now the horror show.

On the radio, every five minutes it seemed, urgent announcers promised listeners they'd have nightmares for a week if they dared set foot inside the theater.

In the newspaper, a classified ad appeared:

LOST OR STRAYED
GIANT UNEARTHLY MONSTER, 7 FT. TALL... IF SEEN, DO
NOT TRY TO CAPTURE, VERY DANGEROUS. CALL
DR. OGRE BANSHEE AT THE SOUTHTOWN THEATER.

During the week my parents took me along to a Julie Andrews movie. In the lobby was something that held me transfixed, so gripped me that my dad had to haul me, heels dragging, into the theater.

A coffin, old and weathered. And closed.

At first I was disappointed, until I saw the sign on the side of the casket:

Quiet Please. Dr. Ogre Banshee Asleep Inside.

It was the longest week in my life, and the night before the show it would have taken more than a closed coffin to give me a good night's sleep.

I flew out of bed early on Saturday morning, skipping *Frankenstein Jr. and the Impossibles* and *Space Ghost,* planning to race down to the theater.

A rake flew into my hand instead.

That was the deal, I knew. I shouldn't have acted so euphoric when I told him.

So I raked, wondering how the yard had grown so much over the summer, wishing we lived in an apartment with hard-drinking men who devoted themselves to cocktail parties and rolled their eyes at the neighborhood's dedication to the care and feeding of its lawns.

It was a minute after noon when I leapt onto my bike and rocketed down to the theater, feeling panicked but still pretty special and full of myself. Of all the kids in town, I had been chosen to be Dr. Banshee's ghost.

When I arrived at the theater, there didn't seem to be anybody around, until I went around back.

A handful of workers were hauling equipment out of a big green truck, wheeling the show into the theater. Lighting gear, black cases with CHASM OF SPASMS stenciled on their sides, unmarked coffins, sharp blades.

And about a half dozen other boys my age, getting fitted for ghost costumes.

My heart plunged.

I saw Don, left my bike under a nearby crabapple tree, the rotten fruit deep at its base, and hustled over to him.

He had a clipboard in hand, pencil jabbing at the paper. "One second there, pal," he said. He probably didn't even remember me. He probably had recruited hundreds of kid ghosts this week alone.

Putting the clipboard down on a trunk, Don looked at me.

"Hey, it's the boy who dared to touch a dead body. Dave, right?"

"Uh huh."

"Thanks for making it. When I saw you the first time, I said to myself, 'Now there's a boy you can count on.' And here you are."

"Sorry I'm late. My dad…"

"No sweat," he said. "We're running a little late ourselves."

"I have a question," I said meekly.

"Shoot, but give me a chance to duck first."

"Okay, uh, what kind of ghost should I be?"

"What *kind* of ghost? How about a dead one?"

"No, that's not what I mean. How long have I been dead? What did I die from? Am I a mean ghost or a happy ghost or..."

Don laughed, although not in a mean way. "Hey, congratulations, kid. You're the first recruit who wondered what his motivation is. You're a regular Marlon Brando."

An unseen voice from inside the truck called out, "Don Mondor, are you out there?"

"Gotta run, kid. The good doctor is calling." Backing away toward the truck, he said, "You're going to make the show tonight, aren't you?"

"Yeah, my dad is going to take me. Wouldn't let me go alone."

"Watch for me. I'll be the one wearing the clodhoppers and the flattop haircut." He turned and pulled himself up into the belly of the truck.

A woman with intensely curled red hair and a bright smile came over and helped me into the ghost get-up and gave me a stack of flyers that said, in shuddering creepy letters, *SPOOK SHOW TONIGHT!*

It was hard to see much through the narrow eye-holes, and it was hot, but I was happy, as I passed out one-sheets to everyone I stumbled into. Because my ghost had motivation, and because soon the orange zombie ticket would be given to me, and I would cross the rickety bridge that led into the dark magic kingdom of the Chasm of Spasms.

•

I didn't know exactly what I was expecting to see, as my dad and I joined the crowd that already circled the theater once and was threatening to spill out into the street.

But as we finally entered the theater and found a pair of seats in the middle of the hall, I felt a little bit of the fizz fading. The theater didn't look like a graveyard, the only spooky touch a backdrop on the stage painted with dancing skeletons and witches on broomsticks cruising by full moons. My seat wasn't much of a coffin either. Just the same old creaky chair with gum stuck under the armrests.

Most of the audience was older than me, high school kids, and they were getting restless. A popcorn container sailed over our heads.

Then…music, a fanfare, a screaming disc jockey rattling off an unintelligible introduction.

The show began under the regular house lights, the brightest graveyard in the world. A comforting light, not a light of fear. It was far darker on the outside.

A magician in a tuxedo appeared from between the curtains. He was short and boyish-looking and was…*smiling*. He peeled off his gloves and flung them high, where they suddenly transformed into a pair of doves.

He materialized bowls of goldfish out of the thin well-lit air. Not piranhas. Goldfish.

He did a picket pocket trick.

A levitation bit.

He brought up a group of kids onto the stage and made them sit down, then somehow caused one of the seats to become so hot that the volunteer shot up to his feet. The audience loved it, but I didn't think it was that funny.

The show was no more fantastic than what I saw on TV every Saturday morning on Mark Wilson's *Magic Land of Allakazam*.

Then there was a twist contest, starring Famous Hollywood Starlet Ronni Dukes. She looked a lot like the woman who helped me into my ghost suit. I sank lower in my seat. I didn't want to see any dance contest unless the contestants were zombies.

I looked around, bored, as the twist contest concluded; it seemed to me that the lights in the theater had dimmed a degree. Maybe not. I wasn't sure.

The winner of the dance contest was a peppy girl with a long blonde ponytail.

"As promised," said the magician, fitting a blindfold over her eyes, "somebody here tonight is going to win a dead body, and it looks like you're our lucky winner, young lady."

Her mouth opened wide. The audience cheered.

I edged forward on my seat, hopeful.

A pair of assistants came out of the wings, carrying something.

"Now the pallbearers are bringing out the coffin," the magician explained, his voice hushed. There were giggles throughout the crowd. The casket in question was all of a foot long, and half that wide.

"Now the coffin is being opened…"

The assistants did as instructed, tilting the casket slightly so that the audience could see inside.

The giggles gathered into a gale of laughter.

The magician shushed them with a finger to his lips, his smile broad.

Inside the coffin was a dead body all right. A chicken's dead body, like the kind mom bought at the supermarket. I slumped down again.

"Now I want you to be a brave girl and *touch* the dead body."

The girl recoiled, but the magician gently took her hand and led it to the open coffin. When her fingers met the surface of the dead bird, she yanked her hand away and let out a yelp.

The crowd howled. I tried not to break out of my horror mood, but I starting laughing, too. It was so dumb.

The lights dimmed again, this time more noticeably. There were shadows in the theater now.

The assistants rolled a table onto center stage. On the slab was a coffin-like box, this one with plenty of room for a regulation-sized human body. The magician led one of the female assistants, who strongly resembled Hollywood Starlet Ronni Dukes, only now she was a blonde instead of a redhead, to the front of the table. He then proceeded to hypnotize her, and once she fell under his spell he commanded her to climb up into the coffin.

When she was safely inside, he shut the lid, then lit a torch and thrust it into one of the holes on the side of the casket, setting the interior of the box on fire.

He let it burn right past the point where I began to feel anxious, and as he rapidly approached the point where I wanted to rush the stage and make him stop, the magician removed the lid. The four sides of the box collapsed, revealing a smoldering skeleton on an altar of fire. Billowing green smoke and red flames engulfed her charred remains.

The audience sat in stunned silence, myself included.

The theater darkened again. Now the shadows were everywhere. "In a very short time," said the magician in a horrifyingly matter-of-fact voice, "every light in this theater will be extinguished. At that time, spirits, spooks and goblins will roam the auditorium. Some of them may come and sit next to you...some will plant cold, icy kisses on your cheeks. Girls, when all the lights go out, you're going to feel a strange invisible hand reach around and caress you in the dark. This side of the audience will feel rats crawl across their legs, and this side over here will feel snakes crawl up the back of their seats and into their laps."

We were sitting in the middle. What would happen to us?

The smile had drained from the magician's face, departing with the light. He continued in an even, quiet voice: "Now my hunchbacked assistant will be bringing out onto this very stage the Frankenstein monster, in person. Do not be alarmed. The monster obeys my every command..."

Under a sickly green spotlight, a hunchback peeked out at the audience from the fringe of the curtains, then turned to the wings, waving his twisted hand, apparently trying to coax someone, something! out onto the stage.

A moment later, there he stood. The Frankenstein monster. Tall, dark and gruesome. I wasn't scared, although my heart seemed to have picked up speed.

The lights dimmed again. Now it was like the last moments before sunset, before the rise of the Lon Chaney, Jr. moon, and the first tide of darkness tugged down away the final pieces of the day.

The hunchback hooked hands with the monster and led him down the stairs to the front rows of the audience.

The Frankenstein monster didn't seem too ghastly, at first. He was like a child.

The hunchback cupped a hand above his own eyes, as if he was searching for...someone. Then he pointed excitedly off toward the left hand aisle, and guided the monster over there. Kids cowered and laughed as they passed by.

Maybe a third of the way up into the audience, the Frankenstein monster suddenly scooped up a kid sitting along the aisle and lumbered back toward the stage. The victim, a teenage boy, squirmed and struggled and made the most awful noises.

Once they were back up on stage, the monster carted the kid to an operating table, which had somehow appeared when everyone was distracted by the action in the audience. The table was draped with a white tablecloth, just brushing the floor of the stage. Igor strapped the kid onto the slab, enclosing his head in a white sack.

"No, no, no," said the magician, striding over to the table. "Leave that boy alone. Frankenstein monster, I command you to take him back to his seat!"

The monster looked at the magician, and at Igor.

Igor now had a glass of bubbling green liquid. He forced the magician to take it, motioning for him to drink, drink Magician, drink.

The tormented magician gazed out at the audience, and at the potion. He lifted it to his lips, then shook his head and held the vial at arm's length. The crowd was bawling at him to drink, drink, drink.

He gulped, winced, then shut his eyes and downed the mysterious liquid in one violent gulp.

The magician stood frozen for a moment, then suddenly clutched his throat. His face contorted, white foam spurting from his mouth. He writhed about the stage, disappearing behind the operating table.

When he reappeared, the magician had vanished. Now he was a doctor, a mad doctor, Dr. Ogre Banshee, with wild hair and savage eyes and feral fangs.

The mad doctor had a meat cleaver with a blade as big as his head.

Now it was very dark.

It happened fast. The doctor attacked the teenager with the cleaver. A few quick hacks and the boy's head fell off, blood gushing all over the white tablecloth.

Girls in the audience were screaming, and the boys weren't laughing anymore.

Darker still.

The Frankenstein monster grabbed the decapitated head by the hair and got a grip on the meat cleaver and shambled back to the stairs, to the floor, and just as he made a lunge toward the audience, there was an intense white flash, blinding me, then all the light in the theater went away.

It was the darkest space I had ever been in.

The theater now felt like a graveyard, and my seat was indeed a coffin. I thought I smelled damp worm-ridden earth.

I believed.

What happened next is, even after all these years, burned into my mind in a phantasmagoric blur.

In the absolute darkness there appeared glowing bats and spiders and ghosts and dancing skeletons, amid a chorus of sirens, rattling chains, and foghorns. The phantoms would appear and wink out, and soar around the theater.

I began to feel strange sensations on my skin. Crawling things. Something touched my arm. Snakes! Something wet brushed my cheek. A ghost kiss! The hair on the back of my neck leapt up, and goose pimples surged over the rest of me.

The dark assault seemed to last for an hour, my mind so overwhelmed I was shaking by the time the manifestations finally ceased and the house lights slowly rose.

Dr. Ogre Banshee had surrendered to the magician. "Everything you have seen here tonight has been the result of stagecraft and trickery," he said. "It is impossible to produce real live ghosts, and our performance was presented all in the spirit of fun." As he trotted off the stage, to big applause and whistles, a movie started on the screen, and the crowd settled down almost immediately. I don't even remember the title. It didn't matter.

David Prill

We snuck out of the theater shortly after the motion picture began. I waited outside the rear of the theater while my dad sat nearby in the car. A light mist was falling, covering Southtown with a suitably eerie sheen.

The crew began to trickle out, loading their gear back into the truck.

Don finally appeared, lugging a black trunk. He was in a twilight world, wearing a grey sweatshirt, dungarees and sneakers…with bolts in his neck, his head flat and boxlike, his face green and scarred.

"Hiya, kid," Don said as he saw me. He tipped up the trunk, resting his arms on top. "So what did you think of the show?"

"It…it was the neatest thing I've ever seen."

"Were you scared?"

"Me? No."

"Right. When the Doc chopped off the kid's head and I snatched it and started into the audience, and the blackout came, you're telling me you're weren't scared?"

"Well, maybe a little."

"Did you laugh?"

"Sure."

"Then we did our job."

I looked at him with intense gravity. "*How did you do it?*"

The monster grinned. "I'm sworn to secrecy. I can't break the code of the magicians."

I knew it was true.

"When are you coming back?" I asked.

"Who knows." He reached into his back pocket and unfolded an orange sheet, showing it to me. The title said:

ROUTE FOR THE DR. OGRE BANSHEE HORROR SHOW
FALL OF 1966.

It showed a list of cities, starting in the Midwest and heading down south, with a theater and a date for each show. There were very few dates that didn't have a town listed alongside them. "If you're down in Waxahacie, Texas on November 30, make sure to stop by and say hi."

"That must be awful tough," I said. "Being away from home all the time like that."

"It's going to be worth it," said Don. "I'm just learning the ropes with the Doc. Someday I'll have my own show. I'm devising a terror levitation that will knock your socks off—with your feet still in them. I'll bring it back here and maybe by then *you'll* be tall enough to play the Frankenstein monster."

"Really? You'd let me?"

"Sure, kid. That's a promise."

A short, slight man came over, still in his tuxedo, a pleased, tired look on his face.

"Hi, son," he said, kneeling down so that we were at eye level. "I'm Dr. Ogre Banshee. Did you enjoy the show?"

"Uh huh." Being inarticulate was often a way of life.

"The kid here was on the ghost squad," said Don. "Remember, the little character actor I told you about?"

"Oh yes," the Doctor said. "Now, there's something I'd like you to have, son. Carry it with you at all times and it will bring you good luck." He sunk his hand into the folds of his fine jacket and produced a single grain of odd, green-tinged rice.

David Prill

•

In spite of the impact that first encounter with the Chasm of Spasms had on me, my young life went on. A year is an eternity to a boy, with holidays to hurdle, running the gauntlet of junior high, a vacation to the Black Hills of South Dakota, Wall Drug, the Passion Play, the Cosmos. I was growing like a stalk of corn. I was beginning to find Superman a little dull.

A certain cruelty, crudity, meanness, had begun to be embraced by the other boys at school. I witnessed two classmates I knew, who had good reputations, taking a girl down a hallway after the first wave of afternoon buses had left and doing things to her I didn't really understand. I wanted to say something, tell them to stop, but she seemed so willing. I wanted to join in, but something held me back. I saw a pair of teachers slam a kid into a locker for spreading rumors that one of them was a drunk. Some longhaired burnout I had never even talked to punched me in the face twice in the middle of a social studies class. Completely unprovoked. It stung, and my eyes filled with tears, but I pretended like I hadn't felt a thing. I heard talk of drug parties. As long as the days sometimes seemed, the world around me was changing very quickly. The chasm of spasms called adolescence.

Looking back, I sometimes wished I had been old enough to run off with the spook show the first time it came to town. The first regret of a series. I collected them all. My life would have been so different had I leapt into the chasm then. To break out of the Midwestern

72

mold, the box where you live, the comfortable, Hush Puppies life, well-worn and predictable. To go off into the wilderness, to act like every day meant something special, to really believe that the unexpected is always possible, to live life as if it mattered.

If I could have taken that step while I was still young enough, strong enough to step away from everything I was taught, to break away for good, things would have been so different.

I'm not sure where the spook shows played in those years. Maybe they came to town on our vacation. Maybe they skipped our town. Maybe my mind was simply elsewhere. I don't know. The night of the Chasm of Spasms remained with me, but it had taken a step back into line with my other memories.

Until the summer of '68.

The summer of love.

The summer of fear.

The summer I began to see that the world wasn't what I had been taught by the kind and gentle teachers at Humboldt Heights Elementary or the teenager wranglers at Penn Junior High.

My family watched Walter Cronkite every night. I saw the body counts and riots. There was a fight in a steaming jungle, and it wasn't the Flash battling Gorilla Grodd, it was something far harder to visualize, to explain in a handful of primary color pulpy panels.

Everything important, in the world at large and small, the true heart of things, seemed to be unspoken, going on out of sight.

Behind the curtains...

David Prill

1968
Tune in, Turn on, Drop Dead

On the day Martin Luther King, Jr. was assassinated, Don Mondor came into my life again.

I was casting my days in loneliness, as my peers drifted off into teenage drugs and teenage sex and teenage rock n' roll that wasn't any good either. The loneliness hurt like a cavity-riddled molar. I was restless. After the news came on the TV about the shooting, I wandered the streets, in the rain, the cold, the despair. I didn't know any better. I didn't know there was a world out there, or least a small dark nook of the world, that would offer me a kind look and an embrace.

It was rainy and I was walking, and I came upon the Southtown Theater.

Standing in the rain, in the street, I stared at the marquee.

BIG HORROR SHOW
DR. SATAN'S SHRIEKS IN THE NIGHT
MATERIALIZATION OF MARILYN MONROE
HOLLYWOOD STARLET RONNI DUKES GO-GO DANCES
IN PERSON — GARGANTA, GIANT GORILLA OF THE
UNIVERSE — 782 POUNDS OF DYNAMITE
8 PM FRIDAY — ONE SHOW ONLY

I smiled, remembering that night only a couple years ago that seemed so far away now.

I wondered what had ever happened to Dr. Ogre Banshee, and Don Mondor, and the Twist.

After another week of ninth-grade detention, I rode my ten-speed down to the theater.

Although it was still a couple of hours until show time, already a line of people snaked around the front of the theater. But I wanted to see what was happening in the back. Right away I spotted Don, as if I was instinctively drawn to him. He was unloading equipment from a small truck and for me it was like no time had passed since my night in the Chasm of Spasms. For him, though, there had no doubt been hundreds if not thousands of shows and towns and little wide-eyed boys in between.

My eyes weren't as wide as they used to be, and as I approached Don I could see that the miles had worn on him, too.

When I got close, he glanced at me but kept working. "Hi, Don," I said.

He stopped, puzzled. "You know me, guy?"

"I was at your show a few years ago. Dr. Ogre Banshee and the Chasm of Spasms. It was great."

"Oh yeah. The Philip Morris show. That was a really good show. Quality stuff."

"So are you Dr. Satan? Is this your show?"

"Nah. This is a Jack Baker outfit. This is a little different situation." He laughed, then looked at me. "Hey, do you want to be in the show?"

"Really?"

"Sure. Come on in. We can always use another cane pole waver."

I followed Don through the rear entrance to the back of the theater.

There were a few people milling around backstage, without any real sense of urgency. A variety of odd-looking objects were scattered across the floor. A series of bright lights was aimed directly onto them.

I picked up something that looked like a large Ping-Pong paddle with a pale green bat painted onto it.

"That's a spook paddle," Don explained, taking it from me. He moved the paddle back and forth, dipping it down and raising it high. "He's flying, right." Now he twisted the paddle, so that the face of the paddle turned toward him. "Now the bat disappears."

Don picked up a cane fishing pole that was longer than me. Paper strips were attached to the end of the pole. "Spook pole," said Don. Waving it vigorously, he said, "It's long enough so that you can get it out over the heads of the audience."

Painted skeletons on black fabric, also affixed to cane poles. "You can run the aisles with these," said Don. "Very effective."

In bins, under the lights, were wet mop strings, popcorn kernels, Ping-Pong balls and rice, all painted pale green.

"What are these for?" I asked.

"In a very short time," Don said in a monotone, "every light in this theater will be extinguished. At that time, spirits, spooks and goblins will roam the auditorium. Some of them may come and sit next to you...some will plant cold, icy kisses on your cheeks. Girls, when all the lights go out, you're going to feel a strange invisible hand reach around and caress you in the dark. This side of the audience will feel rats crawl across their legs, and this side over here will feel snakes crawl up the back of their seats and into their laps."

I couldn't believe it. "No way. That's all there was to it?"

"The power of suggestion is an amazing thing," Don said, scooping up a handful of rice, and letting it stream through his fingers. Then he showed me a large portrait of Marilyn Monroe. "Luminous paint on black canvas. *Voila*. The materialization of Marilyn Monroe."

"Wow."

"Now the important thing, kid, is that when the monster heads down toward the audience, look away. That's when the flash pots will go off, right before the blackout. The flash blinds the audience and charges whatever is coated with the luminous paint. If you don't turn away, you'll be blinded, too."

A young blonde-haired woman in a short gold-speckled sequined dress and white knee-high boots came by. "Have you seen Jack?" she asked.

"No, I haven't seen him since we got here."

"Well he'd better hurry up. The show's supposed to start in fifteen minutes."

I watched her leave until Don poked me on the arm. "When the blackout starts," he said, "I want you to stay with me. Keep your eyes on the floor. There are luminous markers which show us the aisles, the edge of the stage and the wings. I'll tell you which pieces I want. Got it?"

"Got it."

"Jack's here," someone said, and the troupe gathered around an older man with curly white hair and an aging makeup-caked woman in a floor-length fur coat.

"About time," Don said. "The show's going to start in ten minutes."

"So what's the monster tonight?" Jack asked in a slurred voice.

The workers all looked at each other in disbelief.

"I'll go check," Don finally said, and ran out the back of the theater.

Returning a moment later, he said, in a panicky voice, "Jack, it's Garganta, the Giant Gorilla of the Universe!"

Jack nodded calmly, saying nothing, then he turned to his wife. "Margie, give me your fur coat."

She looked at him indignantly. "No goddammit Jack, you're not getting the fur coat *again!*"

It had happened before?

Jack grabbed a handful of fur and tried to pull it off her. Margie fought back. They wrestled with it for awhile, then finally Jack won and took possession of the coat. He and Don fitted it around a thin basketball player-sized fellow with a shock of black hair.

"Now we need something for the head," Jack said.

A few moments of rummaging around backstage before one of the assistants called out, "Hey, look what I found!" Above a cabinet was a moose head, left over from a nature show or a Moose convention or maybe the theater manager just enjoyed the art of taxidermy. The assistant hoisted himself onto the cabinet and detached the head from the wall, and another fellow helped him bring it down and carry it over to their leader.

"Bob, that can't work," said Don. He had a distressed look on his face.

"Sure it will," the assistant replied. He gave a thumbs up sign to the other assistant, and they lifted the moose over their heads and then rammed it against the floor.

One of the antlers snapped off. They lifted the head again and slammed it down again. The other half of the rack broke away. All that was left was a furry head with two little stubs. They fitted it onto the actor's head.

"There you are," said Jack. "Garganta, the Giant Gorilla."

"Jack, that monster looks like shit," Don said. "It's not going to fool anybody."

"Under the green light," Jack said in a knowing voice, "no one will be able to tell the difference."

As the crew resumed their pre-show routine, I asked Don, "What did he mean by that, 'under the green light nobody will be able to tell the difference'?"

"That's what Jack always says. No matter how fucked up something in the show is, he thinks the stage lights will fix it." He rubbed his hands over his face. "Garganta the Giant Gorilla — Jack's wife's fur coat and a moose head with the antlers broken off. 782 pounds of dynamite? 782 pounds of shit. Shit shit shit."

The green light didn't help much.

As I watched from the wings, the crowd began to get rowdy, heaving popcorn containers and pop cups all throughout the miracle bar, the ghost slate and the Dissecto wrist chopper bits, all the lame magic routines in Dr. Satan's repertoire, and a brief go-go dance by Hollywood starlet Ronni Dukes. When Garganta finally made his pathetic appearance, shuffling down toward the audience, some kid jumped on Garganta the Giant Gorilla of the Universe's back. Garganta spun around, trying to pull the kid off him, dislodge him somehow, the fur coat partly slipping off, the moose head twisting around. Finally Garganta freed himself of the pest and staggered back up the stairs to the stage, where he tripped and crawled through the curtains. The crowd hooted and roared.

During the blackout I handed Don paddles as he asked for them and followed him offstage as the screen lit up with the night's bad movie.

"I don't remember the spook show being like this," I told Don as I helped him pack the paddles into a large suitcase.

"They aren't like this," said Don. He glanced around to make sure nobody was within earshot. "The Chasm of Spasms was a legitimate show. This is an *illegitimate* show. Jack used to be a good showman. He put on a first-rate performance. He cared about what he was doing. Now…" He waved a hand, making a disgusted noise. "Garganta in a fur coat. Jesus."

"What are you going to do?"

Another surreptitious glance around. "I've got big plans, kid. At the end of this tour I'm going to take my own spooker on the road: *Dr. Morbid and His Horror Chamber of Blood and Doom*. It will be top quality stuff. Ronni is coming with me. What do you think?"

"I'd go see it."

"You should be part of it."

"What do you mean?"

"Go on tour with us."

"I can't even drive a car yet."

"How old are you?"

"Thirteen. I'm just a kid."

"Well when you get old enough then. Deal?"

"Deal."

"Why don't you hang around after we get packed up? Ronni and I are going out for coffee. Join us if you'd like."

"Really?"

"You got something better to do?

"Well no…"

"Then you're coming."

After trucks were loaded and locked, the rest of the crew headed to the nearest bar, Jack, his wife and her reclaimed fur coat disappeared for parts unknown, and Don, Ronni and I walked over to the Southtown bowling center, which was located across the parking lot from the theater.

We sat at the counter, Ronni with a mug of coffee, Don with a bottle of beer, me between them with an Orange Crush, as the sounds of pins getting pummeled echoed around us.

"Guys like Jack Baker are killing the spook show business," Don said. "They're burning up perfectly good territory. See, a second-rate spooker comes to town, does a crummy show, leaves the audience feeling pissed off and cheated, and so the next spook show that arrives has a real hard time getting booked."

"So why are you working for him?" I asked.

Don shrugged. "The money. This is Jack's first unit. He's got eight units playing every night. He's raking it in. It won't last, but right now he's doing great box office. It's the theater owners' biggest night of the week when we hit town. And before I started in the business you could make even more by bicycling the show. That was back when it was more common for towns to have several movie theaters. You'd play the movie at one house while you did the show in the other. Then you'd switch. You could have shows all night if you had enough theaters and a good double feature, just by staggering the starting times. Add it up yourself. A few guys retired rich men after playing the circuit during the heyday of spook shows." He slugged down his beer.

"At least we're not with Kara-Kum anymore," Ronni said.

Don chortled. "The mighty Kara-Kum. Christ. Kid, you should have seen him. A short Middle Eastern guy in a turban with a phony jewel in the middle. The Crawling Thing From Planet #13. A blob of jelly covered with luminescent paint. It just sat there on the stage and didn't do shit. Christ, that was awful."

"He has great advertising at least," said Ronni.

"Kara-Kum has the best promotion gimmicks of anyone," said Don. "Beautiful window cards, one sheets, really cool trailers…"

"And no show."

"You got it."

"Others imitate…Kara-Kum originates."

Don started laughing again.

Pins clattered onto the plywood.

"The whole field is going to hell," said Don. "Bill Neff must be rolling over in his coffin."

"Who is Bill Neff?" I asked.

Don looked at me with raised eyebrows. "Who is Bill Neff. Why Bill Neff taught me everything I know." His voice got sad and he clutched his beer glass. "Bill died last year. A stroke."

"He drank himself to death," Ronni said to me in an aside.

Silence, then Don's face lightened again. "But anyway, Bill put on a great show. He called it the Madhouse of Mystery. Lots of humor, which is very important, you know. You have to have it. Because you say anything to get people in the theater, *anything,* no matter how outrageous, to get fannies in the seats. Then you have a problem. They're expecting something incredible…"

"Like Garganta, the Giant Gorilla of the Universe," I said.

"Exactly. And once they're there in the theater, you've got to figure out a way to keep them entertained so they don't want to kill you when they leave. If you can make them laugh, entertain them a little bit, they won't mind that you overdid the ballyhoo. And Bill Neff always made sure people left the theater happy."

The TV on the wall behind the counter showed rioters burning cars on the streets of a big city.

"Shit, that's a damn shame," said Don. Another hearty swig. "We played Memphis last month. They hit Garganta over the head with a baseball bat. And now this. Unbelievable."

"They were pawing at me," Ronni said.

"Those damn hillbillies."

"I wouldn't go back there for any money."

"It's a weird time to be in the spooker business, kid, with all that's happening in the world," Don said. "Boys not much older than yourself are dying overseas, and we're pretending to slaughter people on the stage. We were in Chicago during the Democratic convention, trying to unload the trucks outside a theater not far from the convention center. So out of one eye you're seeing protesters raising hell and getting their brains beat in by the cops, and out of the other eye you're trying to unpack your spook paddles and your luminous rice and your guillotine. A couple of hippies came by and looked at us kinda funny and said, Hey man, far out. What's happening here, man? I told them it was a scare-in and gave them a pair of free passes to the show. They ran screaming out of the theater when the blackout started — must have thought they were having a bad trip." Don got up. "Gotta use the can," he said, and headed off into the dimness of the bowling alley.

I was alone with Ronni Dukes. I had never sat alone, sharing a drink, with a grown up woman that wasn't my mom. And as I sneaked a glance at her as she sipped her coffee, she was about as grown up as I imagined a woman could get.

"So, hon," she said, looking at me with a sweet smile, "how come you're all alone on a Friday night. Don't you have a girlfriend?"

My eyes dropped down. "No...no."

"Not many friends either."

"I had one, he lived right across the street from me. We were walking to school one day, talking about what we wanted to be when we grew up, and he said he wanted to be an accountant."

"The poor boy."

"A lot of the kids where I live are like that."

"So what do you want to do?"

"Be part of a spook show...I mean, a spooker."

"It's not an easy life. You're in a new town almost every night. You look at the people in the audience and you know that after the lights go up they've got familiar beds to sleep in, a house with warm lights and a home-cooked meal and a town they know and love to wake up to in the morning."

"Why do you do it, then?" I asked.

"Because it's show business. It's all I know. I'm not the happy housewife type. Don is a great guy. He's starting to drink some, ever since we signed on with Baker. I think Baker's sloppiness kills him. He really wants his own show. He wants to do it right, to be another Bill Neff. And he'll make it, too. I only hope it's not too late."

"What do you mean?"

"Oh, TV is hurting us pretty bad. We're tied to movie theaters, and movie theaters are going through hard times right now. They're putting in wide screens. Only the old theaters have stages big enough to put on a quality show, and a lot of those have gone out of business. You can rig up a portable stage, but that limits how elaborate a show you can put on. It's getting harder and harder to bring in enough money to make it worthwhile."

I thought about this for a moment, then said, "Can I ask you a question?"

"Certainly, dear."

"What movies have you been in?"

Ronni smiled coyly. "What makes you think I've been in the movies?"

"You're a Hollywood starlet."

"I lived in Hollywood for four months when I was eight years old. And hon, you do think I'm a star, don't you?" She leaned toward me, her hand on my knee.

I blushed. I could feel the heat on my cheeks, on my neck, everywhere, and wished I had a free blindfold for those who embarrass easily.

"See?"

Just then Don came back and said it was time for them to get back on the road.

I didn't want them to leave. I wanted to go with them.

"See you next time we're in town, kid," Don said, shaking my hand. "You can be part of the show again."

Ronni leaned over and kissed me on the cheek, another milestone. I smelled her perfume, her hair, her soul. She was beautiful and mysterious and defied death and danced the go-go every night on the stage. She was everything I thought a woman should be.

For a long time afterward, whenever the discussion among the kids at school would drift to their favorite movie stars, I would always answer, "Ronni Dukes."

•

This encounter with the Shrieks in the Night, as second-rate a show as it was, had a profound effect on me. I felt like I had found a home. The first time Don and Ronni had come to town, with the Chasm of Spasms, even though I was thrilled and amazed and needed the free cough drops if you scream too much, I was too young to appreciate it—now I was old enough to appreciate it, but too young to do anything about it.

But I was so proud. I had worked my first spooker. Even more importantly, I felt connected to Don and Ronni in a strange and intense way. It felt so comfortable being around them, as if we had been friends for years. I often had dreams of being in an unfamiliar place, communing with people who knew my deepest thoughts and needs, while the people at home, my family and friends, people who lived right at hand, whom I saw every day, simply didn't know me.

Maybe the next time they came to town I would have my driver's license. Maybe by then I would be old enough to do something about it.

David Prill

1972
Dr. Morbid and I'm Not Feeling Much Better Myself

The isolation I was feeling was like an unshakable tether, the distance between myself and my peers at school and in my neighborhood only increasing. After suffering through the horrors of *Signal 30* and *For Want of a Seat Belt* I finally won my driver's license, but soon learned that the car couldn't take me far enough away. Maybe I was just another spoiled baby boomer who brooded when life didn't cater to him. I had the luxury to be alienated. My parents grew up during the Depression, held steadfast through a world war and came out of it all jitterbugging. But they had a cause, a common bond, a home.

Mine was an odd generation. Too young to be hippies, yet growing up in their wake. Only the most base aspects of their world seemed to filter down to us. The psychedelic billboard highlights of drugs and sex. Ideals were a tougher sell.

I drove the streets in my parents' discarded Ford Galaxie rust machine, searching. I knew there was a bigger world out there, but I was beginning to get the idea that it would be as closed to me as everything else seemed to be. I once had a dream about a flaming tomahawk spinning toward me from the dark, and this seemed to be the signature of every encounter I had, every attempt I made to reach across the divide.

So I drove. It was easier than walking and you didn't have to be confronted with every detail of a world that felt like a barbed-wire rail.

The Last Horror Show

My town had changed. There was less separation between it and the city at large; it was assuming more characteristics of the city, and losing its individuality. Becoming bigger, brighter, noisier, faster. Roads were widened and trees were cleaved from the earth. Burn barrels were banned. A neighbor family who kept chickens in their backyard were told to get rid of them or get fined. They moved to a small town up north instead, taking the chickens with them. When I was a small boy, one of the dads on our block loaded all the kids within shouting range onto a short flatbed trailer, hopped aboard a tractor and hauled us down some of the busiest streets in town and nobody honked or gave us the finger. I couldn't imagine that happening now.

I found myself cruising past the Southtown Theater more and more frequently, slowly circling, eyeing the marquee, praying for some lurid come-on, some sign that the world in my heart had returned, free smelling salts in the lobby, tough bodyguard available for those too frightened to go home alone.

Summers that were once as distinct as fingerprints now began to blur and congeal. The week after the Fourth of July, which I spent watching distant fireworks from my closed and curtained bedroom window, it was rainy and I was driving, this time out on the highway on the fringes of town, one step from the trailer parks I figured were in my future, when I saw the sign outside the Lucky Twin Drive-In.

Parked in the rain, along the muddy shoulder, I tumbled out of the car and gaped at the marquee.

FRANKENSTEIN IN PERSON
DR. MORBID'S HORROR CHAMBER OF BLOOD AND DOOM
HOLLYWOOD STARLET RONNI DUKES DISCO DANCES
PLUS 3 FRIGHT FLICKS
FRIDAY NIGHT — ONE SHOW ONLY

As I stood there, getting drenched, I felt elated and sad and relieved.

But what had happened? Why wasn't Don playing the Southtown Theater? Why was he out here at the Lucky Twin, in the rain? How could you do a spook show at a drive-in? How could you stage a blackout in the middle of a gravel lot? Don must have figured out a way to do it. I was eager to learn his secrets.

The idea of visiting a drive-in alone didn't thrill me. I knew it would make me painfully self-conscious. What kind of weirdo goes to a drive-in by himself? I never thought I would be in a position like that. I always figured I would go with a carload of friends, sneaking a few extra bodies in the trunk.

Lucky Twin — four-leaf clovers in green neon, letters in white, on the black backside of each of the facing screens. Once I remember peeking at fascinatingly trashy women in a prison film through the rearview mirror while a mediocre Steve McQueen auto racing movie filled the night sky before us.

The last time I had been at the Lucky Twin was to see a Hammer Films double feature, *Frankenstein and the Monster From Hell* and *Captain Kronos: Vampire Hunter*. With my father. There was no other option, if I wanted to see the films, which I did with an aching desire.

That was awkward enough. In theory I could find someone to go with me to the spook show; some of the burnouts had acted friendly toward me at the end of the last school year, although it was a social circle I didn't particularly care to frequent, and they were as content and dreamless as anyone.

I decided then to go to the drive-in alone. It was the first time I belligerently didn't care what other people thought about my behavior. Anyway, the spook show world, in the persons of Don and Ronni Dukes the Hollywood Starlet, was a world I didn't want to share with anybody.

In the days leading up to the arrival of the Horror Chamber of Blood and Doom, I kept to the streets as much as possible, hoping for a glimpse of Don or Ronni or one of their confederates as they doused the town with their colors, battered us with their ballyhoo.

But as always happened, I woke up one morning midweek and like an overnight snowfall, the lurid window cards, one sheets and full-size posters appeared on every exposed surface in town. I rejoiced; the town belonged to me again, was made over in their image, in my imagination, if only for a few short days and one wonderfully blood-chilling night.

It rained all day Friday, a steady cold rain under solid dead flesh skies. While it created the proper mood, I worried about the show.

I headed down to the Lucky Twin long before dusk. The rain was coming down as hard as it had all day. The gates were still closed, so I parked in the puddles and hiked through the weeds and mud along the white fence on the perimeter of the lot until I saw Don and Ronni.

They were on top of the cinder block concession stand, wrapped up in yellow rain slickers, rigging up some fright-inducing apparatus. I ducked between the fence rails and tramped over to them.

It was like we had just said goodbye at the bowling alley last night. They descended from above like the gods I felt they were and greeted me with high warmness, Don vigorously shaking my hand, Ronni hugging the breath out of me. I felt like I had finally crossed over, from being just another kid who liked to hang around a show to a real friend, a familiar face they looked forward to seeing when they were on the endless road.

"You did it!" I gushed. "You have your own show. Dr. Morbid. The Horror Chamber of Blood and Doom. This is so great."

"Thanks, kid," Don said, and while I could tell his pride was genuine, there was also an undercurrent of sadness in his voice, as if this wasn't exactly what he had dreamed about when he was learning from Bill Neff and suffering through Jack Baker and Garganta. I don't know how I knew this from his simple reply; I just felt it, sensed it.

They had both aged noticeably since our last meeting. Don's hairline had begun to recede, and he had gained weight. His face, particularly his cheeks and nose, were flushed red. Ronni still looked lovely, beneath her slicker, from the hints of her disco dress that I could see, her hair feathered stylishly although mashed down by her wet hood at the moment. But there were lines in the corners of her eyes and mouth. Her hands were more wrinkled than supple. Her face had begun to sag, her once defined cheekbones filled up with flesh. The way she walked and moved seemed different, too. More tired. The road, the dance crazes, had taken their toll.

"Where are the trucks?" I asked, looking around the lot.

"This is it," Don said with a short laugh, pointing at the rusty blue Pontiac parked alongside the concession stand. "It's easier to travel light," he explained. "Hauling a ton of equipment around the country just creates headaches. I don't need a lot of gimmicks to rock an audience's primal-spinal."

"Last time you were in town you told me I could work the show," I said. "What can I do?"

"Well let's think about this for a minute," Don drawled. "Don't need any cane pole wavers at a drive-in. I can always use an extra monster — some of the drive-in crew are playing monsters, but their hearts aren't always in it. They need a lead dog. Feel like scaring people tonight, kid?"

"Sure. What kind of monster?"

"Frankenstein, Dracula, the Wolfman, take your pick."

"The Count, please."

"Good deal. Ronni will help you get made up in a little while." Don glanced at the skies. "That damn rain. It was supposed to have cleared up by sunset. We can dance around it, at least. Come on, we've got some work to do yet before the folks start showing. It'll be dark before we know it."

I followed Don up the ladder to the roof of the concession stand, Ronni behind me.

They had strung up a small tarpaulin shelter behind the witchy backdrop. We crouched low and entered between the flaps. Inside were monster suits, tins of black and white shoe polish, makeup jars, Day-Glo show flyers, three camping stools, and a pot of coffee.

Don poured for everyone. I had tried coffee only a couple of times, and didn't like it. Now I gratefully accepted the mug. It was hot and I was cold and I wanted to feel like I was part of the regular crew.

Looking at Ronni, Don said, "My best guess is that we'll run *She-Freak* first, take the stage around midnight, then give them a *Blood Feast* and *Color Me Blood Red* double dip. If the rain doesn't break until later, we'll get started after *Blood Feast,* probably around 2 am."

She nodded. "Sounds like a plan."

They didn't even ask me if I could stay out that late, and I took it as a sign of respect. They knew I wouldn't have come out here if I wasn't serious.

We finished setting up the show, then retreated to the tent as the early birds arrived and took spots on the ramps nearest the giant curved screen. Every so often, one of us would peek out and report back on how full the lot was becoming.

"Why are you playing a drive-in?" I asked Don, trying to sound upbeat.

He didn't appear to take offense. "The last theater we played, we ended up owing *them* money," he said. "That goddamn manager charged us for everything except the rats in the dressing rooms. I like drive-ins. Most drive-in owners appreciate a good showman.

They're doing well enough that they don't have to gouge us. We provide everything, even the movies. Everything is under our control. We split the ad costs, and I throw in a little extra for the drive-in employees who help us, and everybody is happy. A triple feature with our monster show. It's usually their highest gross of the week."

Don lifted back the tent flap. "Look, pouring rain and there are cars lined up out along the highway waiting to get in to see us, just like the old days at the movie houses. We're not getting rich off drive-ins, because we just have the one unit right now, but we're doing okay. I have all kinds of ideas that I want to try out in this venue. You're dealing with a captive audience — five hundred cars or five hundred theater seats, doesn't matter. The difference is that it's easier to get them to open their wallets in the safety of their automobiles. That's a fact. Unless people stop driving their cars, which will never happen, there's no reason why drive-ins shouldn't be around forever."

Just then a stocky man in a crewcut and horn-rimmed glasses ventured up to the tent. He had his blue Twins cap pulled down low over his eyes. He looked worried. "You're not going to have to cancel the show, are you?"

Don grinned at the man. "Why Mr. Bunting, it would take a tornado to keep the Horror Chamber of Blood and Doom from scaring the daylights out of your customers, and even then we'd find a way of incorporating it in the show."

The theater manager appeared relieved but uncertain. "You can do the show in the rain?"

"Show *She-Freak* and keep on showing the rest of the films until the rain stops. Have you heard the forecast?"

"The front was supposed to have moved through an hour ago."

"Then we'll be out there hacking up your customers in no time. Send up your boys who are going to play monsters halfway through the first movie. We'll handle everything else."

"I hope you're right. That's a pretty fair crowd out there for this weather. Would hate to have them bail out early and miss out on all those concession sales."

"Now don't you worry about a thing. I haven't had a rain-out yet and I don't plan on starting tonight."

The evening's program started right on schedule. Just as Don had predicted, the rain petered out a few minutes into *She-Freak*. "I'm going down and get a genuine Smithfield barbecue sandwich and a Chilly Dilly pickle," he said. "You want one, Ronni?"

"Better not. Maybe after the show."

"Kid?"

I nodded. "Sure." Tried not to sound too eager, but I hadn't eaten anything since a bowl of soggy Crispy Critters at breakfast.

Don slipped out of the tent, leaving Ronni and me alone. I had replayed the last time we were alone dozens of times since that night at the bowling alley. I was older now, straddling boyhood and manhood, and even though there was an awkward silence between us after Don left it was thrilling to realize there was something to be awkward about.

"So how have you been doing, hon?" Ronni asked. "It's been awhile."

"Okay, you know," I stumbled. "You look nice."

Ronni fussed with her hair. "Oh, thanks. I feel like a drowned bat…"

A pretty bat, I thought.

She glanced at the tent flap, then at me. "You always look so different each time we come through town. You seem so much older this time, so serious."

Now it was my turn to look away. "I'm real happy for Don. His own show and everything. It must be great."

Ronni leaned closer, like the time she did at the bowling alley, but now there anxiety on her face. She wasn't trying to tease me, she was confiding to me like a friend. "I'm worried about him. His drinking has gotten worse since we started on the drive-in circuit. I don't know if it's the extra responsibility of running his own show instead of just cashing a paycheck, or if he sees Bill Neff looking over his shoulder or what."

"It couldn't have been easy," I said, "being driven out of the movie houses like that."

"It was a bad time. It was all he knew, all he had prepared for his whole life. Then it was over, just like that. We didn't expect it, at least not that fast. We had to scramble to stay afloat."

"What happened to all the spook shows, the Chasm of Spasms, the Shrieks in the Night, the Crawling Thing From Planet #13?"

"Some made it, some went away. Some operators drifted back to straight magic, or signed on with circuses. You can still draw kids for a Saturday matinee monster show, but these days a good first-run movie will do as well as a late-night spook show. People's tastes have changed. The drive-ins are still good, for now, so a lot of the ghostmasters have moved into that market. It's hard to put on a decent show, though, at a drive-in. There's Dr. Franklin's Spooks on the Loose—he uses a flatbed trailer for a stage, a top-notch outfit, but there are just as many scam artists as there ever were and they're burning up territory just as fast as always."

"So what are you going to do?"

Ronni smiled. "Keep dancing." She touched my arm. "I'm sorry, hon. Look at your face. I don't mean to worry you. Don's always got something cooking in that half-baked brain of his. We'll survive."

The Hollywood starlet who could glimpse into my soul. I didn't like what I was hearing, or what she must have seen. I wasn't quite ready to follow them, not quite. It would just take a little longer. Wait another day. I was so close. I wanted to graduate from high school at least, then it would be the right time. Then I would have my feet under me. Then I would understand better. I knew I was scared, afraid of what my parents might do or say, afraid to fail, afraid of change, afraid that things would stay the same, painting alibis on cane poles to wave at myself when things got too dark.

Don seemed to have been gone a long time. When he returned from his mission, he was different somehow. The tension behind his smile as he managed the theater manager had been reined in. He was hugging a paper sack with a stain at the bottom, grinning madly. I snuck a glance at Ronni. She didn't look happy. She said nothing to him.

Don handed me a package wrapped in white paper. "Now this isn't just any barbecue sandwich, kid, this a Smithfield barbecue sandwich. Ask for it by name next time you visit the concession stand at your local drive-in theater."

I was feeling uncomfortable, the first time since I had known them. What was going on? I didn't know.

The movie began, as I wolfed my sandwich, waiting for the vampire transformation. I could hear voices reverberating, calliope music, but I couldn't make out anything distinct. But it did seem to break whatever uneasy spell had crept between the flaps. Dr. Morbid and his lovely assistant tidied themselves up in front of the mirror. Don fussed with some hidden compartment in his beautiful tuxedo. Ronni worked to make sure very little was hidden.

"Let's get you fixed up," she said, bringing the makeup box over to where I was sitting. She unscrewed the lid on a small jar of Griffin all-white shoe polish, dipped her fingers in, scooped up a palm full, and gently slapped it onto my cheek. It felt cool, her hand warm. She continued to apply it, covering my face in white.

Next, she took black shoe polish and slicked back my hair, which hadn't been cut in months. She outlined my eyes with the black, then dribbled red goop from the corners of my mouth to my chin.

After she fitted the plastic fangs into my mouth, she stood back and studied her creation carefully for a moment, then defied convention by lending me a hand mirror.

"Good evening, Count Alucard," Don said, with an approving smile, and I dug the reference.

I thought I looked cartoony and garish, but Ronni said exaggeration was necessary so that the audience could make out my features from a distance. Don helped me into a shiny stained black cloak and I was ready to ravage.

The other monsters joined the party shortly afterwards, three pimply and gawky boys the same age as me. I recognized them from school, although they weren't in my ever-shrinking circle. I think they lived in the duplexes that lined Lyndale Avenue, what passed for the town's rough, cigarette-sneaking, gobbing-on-freshly-mowed-lawns neighborhood. After they were properly outfitted, Don gave us instructions on what to do and when to do it, then as *She-Freak* reached its thrilling climax and the first intermission began, he and Ronni left the tent, pinning back the flap slightly so that we could hear our cues.

Stretch your legs now while the stretchin's good.

It's time to stretch and fetch, see what's cookin at our refreshment counter. You'll find your favorite foods and beverages plus many new goodies to tempt your appetite and add to your evening's pleasure. Everything is the finest quality, so treat yourself...now

"Shit, did you see her?" the Wolfman growled, gawking out the tent opening. "I'd like to get my hands on that piece of pussy-ass."

My hands clenched on reflex, nails digging into my palms.

"Shit, man, she's old enough to be your mom," the Frankenstein monster grunted.

"I don't care. I want her, man."

I stood up, glaring at the werewolf.

"So who are you supposed to be?" he asked, the insult bare in his voice.

"Count Dracula," I said, thankful the topic of conversation had shifted, but still desiring to choke him until his eyes got buggy.

The Mummy, who had been silent until now, said, "You look like a dope."

Ignoring the slight, I tried to make an entreaty to my fellow monsters. "Look guys," I said, "we need to plot out how we're going to do this, the finest way to creep out the audience. I was thinking we could pair up, two monsters are scarier than one…"

"You should have seen what Cheryl Crumley was wearing at the game. You could see right through her shirt. Her nips were sticking out and everything."

"…but now I'm wondering maybe if it would be wiser if we came at 'em from different directions, create the illusion of a slavering horde. And let's not forget about our motivation, how we monsters from very different backgrounds joined forces and why we're about to go on a murderous rampage…"

"She's hot. I did her once."

"You liar."

"Could happen."

"It'll never happen."

"…important to stay in character. These people paid good money and we need to give them our very best effort…"

"I did Mandy Ryerson."

"No way."

"She's a cheerleader."

"I know who she is. She's also two years older than you. I can't believe what a little liar you are."

"I ain't lying. She was babysitting at our neighbor's. I dropped by to borrow a cup of pussy."

"…all we can do is try to live up to the memory of the great Bill Neff…"

"So, the asshole's a queer…"

Ach, hello der. Here is a demonstration of my new inwention, da goodies machine. Special for patrons of dis drive-in, the machine turns out delooscious hot doggies, vun after de udder, und thirst qvenching zodas also, gives popcorn of de most tasty kind, plain und buttered, candy too, crunchy und dandy, shteaming hot coffee, und ice cream too, dese goodies are at our schnack bar, chust waiting for you, mmmmmmmmm…

Directly above the hot doggies and the shteaming hot coffee, Dr. Morbid's Horror Chamber of Blood and Doom had begun.

The only problem was I couldn't see the show, and could barely hear it. Disappointing. I was dying to see Don on center stage, share in his dark dream. But it was a fair trade. I had crossed that magic line from audience to participant, and I wasn't going back.

About ten minutes into the show, rain began to lightly patter the roof of our makeshift shelter. In the distance, the sky rumbled.

It'll stop soon, I thought.

But it didn't. The rain grew louder, the sky-shaking thunder closer. The tent suddenly lit up, and I didn't think it was from a flashpot.

Ronni appeared at the tent opening, breathing hard, rain flattening her disco curls, and said, "We're going to cut the show short, and skip the dismembering. Wait for my second scream, then come running." She dashed back to the stage.

The original plan called for an elaborate operating table sequence, the conclusion of which had the monsters barging in and tearing the victim limb from limb. Each monster was to grab their designated limb and head down toward the audience, who were grouped together in front of the concession stand, just as the stage lights were extinguished. Once on the ground, the monsters were to shamble around the lot pounding on car hoods. It wasn't a real blackout, but Don said it had proven surprisingly effective.

The first scream.

They must be improvising, I thought. Dr. Morbid must have turned his sights to his lovely assistant.

Another scream.

I led the charge. The other monsters were still sitting on their misshapen hands. "Come on!" I yelled at them, catching the torn sleeve of the Frankenstein monster and dragging him outside.

We charged the stage in the deluge. I felt my face melting almost immediately. My eyes began stinging. I tried to get a grasp of the situation.

Dr. Morbid had his lovely assistant splayed across the operating table, hands locked around her slender throat.

Then the doctor abruptly released her, whirling to face us. He held up his arms in self-defense, then scrambled away from the table and made for the ladder. That was it. We were supposed to chase him down like the mad doctor he was.

I started after Dr. Morbid, then glanced back and saw that my fellow monsters were more interested in his lovely assistant.

Thunder cracked right overhead.

"Down the ladder!" I wailed at them, shoving them toward the edge of the roof.

The wind rose, billowing my cape.

Wiping the shoe polish out of my eyes, I gazed out across the drive-in lot. It was only about a third full, a swarm of red taillights gathered down by the gate. The rain was coming down like the heart of a snake throw. Even a Drizzle Gard wouldn't have been much help.

Just as the monsters started descending the makeshift staircase, Ronni hit a switch down by her feet, cutting the stage lights.

Blackout.

And at that same moment, a great light.

Flashpots weren't that bright, and didn't pack that big of a wallop.

I was told it was lightning later, after I regained consciousness. At the time I thought it was part of the show. Some new bit Don had invented to scare the yell out of the drive-in crowd.

Ronni was closer to the point of impact than me. I remember the light, the feeling of being airborne. Don told me later that the paramedics took one look at my face and what was left of my makeup and thought I was a goner.

•

The Last Horror Show

Remember to replace your speaker on its post and be sure the cord is clear of the door handle. Good night.

•

News of my evening at the Horror Chamber of Blood and Doom didn't win me any fans at home, particularly since I had somehow neglected to mention my plans to anyone. After a precautionary overnight stay in the hospital, I was sent packing, feeling like a 782-pound gorilla had pedaled a bicycle across my back. I was grounded, gladly, and imagined Don saying that if I had been grounded before the show, the lightning wouldn't have knocked me on my ass.

It was late afternoon and I was taking a painkiller-induced nap, when she appeared at my bedside.

Had to be a dream. Because she had been in my dreams so many times before.

Even behind her bandages, her eyes shone and even in my delirium my heart started pumping hard.

Her hips began moving awkwardly, a stilted, pained version of the Twist.

I thought I saw a smile.

She moved closer and touched my face with a cool hand.

I reached for her other hand, and as our fingertips met she gathered me in and held on tight.

It was so comforting, and so wonderful, and I quickly drifted back into sleeping.

When I woke again I was alone.

Alone.

David Prill

Returned to another world, a world that should get lost, a smorgasbord of boredom, every banality in the book, a world so dull that only yawns can describe it, where you pay a price for everything.

1973
Sex at the Snack Bar

The lightning didn't hurl me clear of the spookers, it drew me closer, like a magnetic charge, the power of the strike firing my desire.

It was my last year of high school.

I was ready.

I felt like this was something I had been preparing for all my life, as if I was being schooled to scare. There were too many coincidences to think otherwise. Nothing else in my short life had felt so right, had come together so cleanly, so perfectly, had filled me with such hope.

It was the highest, coolest calling.

I was ready.

I didn't know the day or the hour when Don and Ronni would return to my town, with their paneled station wagon of terror. It didn't matter. I would remain vigilant until that day came, the luminous grain of rice that Dr. Ogre Banshee bestowed upon me so many midnights ago squeezed tightly in the center of my palm.

The Lucky Twin Drive-In became my second home.

I spent the first month of summer there, parking off on the fringes, as far from the other cars as possible, not wanting to mingle with those whose only purpose was an evening's diversion. I wandered the lot during the feature presentations, as I had wandered the streets of my town so many nights before. My world seemed to be collapsing in on itself, as if I was homing in on my final goal.

I felt safe at the Lucky Twin. I got acquainted with the staff and eventually was talked into taking a job. It was either that or a restraining order. I did everything, from running the projector to taking admissions at the gate to manning the snack bar. Warming up those week-old delooscious hot doggies for the umpteenth time, I saw bits and pieces of many movies, mostly bad, but not in an entirely bad way. I was beginning to understand the distinction.

The Death Curse of Tartu. The Pigkeeper's Daughter. The Godmonster of Indian Flats.

My parents' concern over my whereabouts and possible unstable mental state turned to a kind of reserved joy when I revealed to them I had taken a full-time position in the entertainment industry. I didn't go into the details and they were happy about that, too.

I kept a watchful eye on the coming attractions reels, screening them in the daylight as soon as they were delivered, hoping for some urgent transmission from Dr. Morbid. Some hint that soon tongues would be ripped out by creatures from the lower world, awful death rattles would be heard, fifty unearthly wonders, not a film but live, one thousand times scarier than anything ever here, fright insurance available for all.

One humid night in early August, Mr. Bunting, the Lucky Twin's manager, caught me brushing the dust, dirt and hair off a platter of unbaked pretzels which I had accidentally dropped on the floor. I froze, afraid I was in grave trouble, picturing a future of lurking outside the drive-in fence.

"What's going on here?" he asked.

"Uh…nothing."

"You dropped the pretzels on the floor, and now you're trying to clean them so they can be cooked up and served to our patrons. Am I right?"

"Yes, Mr. Bunting," I confessed.

I was about to offer an apology, one thousand times more sincere than any apology ever heard, when Mr. Bunting got all smiles and said, "Good job, kid."

A little while later he returned with an armful of blue and red booklets. One said, "Knowledge for Men," the other "Knowledge for Women." A scientific nude outline, with just enough detail to make you want to open the book, graced the cover of each.

"You just got a promotion, fella," Mr. Bunting said, shoving the books at me.

"What are they?"

"A Mom and Dad promotion is coming through tonight. They're going to have the books on sale during intermission. Two bucks apiece. Three bucks if they buy them both."

"What do you mean, 'Mom and Dad'?"

"You know, the Kroger Babb racket. Birth of babies, sex hygiene, strictly educational of course."

After Mr. Bunting departed, I thumbed through the skinny little booklets.

Male sex anatomy.
Causes of impotency in men.
Female sex anatomy.
The female menstrual cycle.
Typical questions a child might ask.
Where do babies come from? They grow inside mothers.
Where did you get me, mother? You grew inside me.

Where do hospitals get babies? They don't get babies, they help mothers.

I shrugged and stacked the booklets on the edge of the counter.

Shortly before the gates opened, I poured the popcorn kernels and oil into the popper, and flipped the switch. The popper began heating up. I filled the coffee urn and turned it on. I sliced buns and felt sad.

As dusk breached the day, the customers, mostly kids my age, began streaming into my realm. I kept my head down, not wanting to make eye contact with them. I wished I was in the solitude of the projection shack. Here, I couldn't even watch the movie.

Charleston Chew, Bubbs Daddy and Bonomo Turkish Taffy.

Fanta and Yoo-Hoo.

Hairless pretzels and frankfurters aged to perfection.

Soon the crowds retreated to their cars as the screen teemed with light.

I refilled the popper and got another batch of the devil's brew cooking. I went to the bathroom. I read "The Festival," from an H. P. Lovecraft paperback collection I had picked up from Shinder's newsstand earlier in the day.

I roamed out to the front windows, where I could get an unobstructed view of the movie.

A fifty-foot-high pregnant belly held my attention briefly. The camera drifted down, down…

Then the movie stopped.

The screen went dark.

Too soon for intermission.

I thought there was a technical problem.

Suddenly, a pair of white spots hit a low platform set up in front of the screen tower. I hadn't noticed it before. A man occupied center stage. He began speaking into a microphone, his voice distorted as it warbled through the cheap speaker nested in the corner of the concession stand ceiling.

"In a few moments we'll continue on and present those very important and vital medical sequences, the pictures that you've been hearing and reading so very much about. Tonight you're going to see something perhaps you never even dreamed was possible to produce for the American screen. You're going to see the actual birth of babies, both natural birth, caesarean section, and then the actual birth of twins. And we do trust that you will receive them in the manner in which we present them, as educational and instructive motion pictures. But it is a little bit bold, and a lot of people actually pass out while viewing it. If you're going to pass out, or you feel like you're going to pass out, why please send someone into the snack bar, so they can come to your aid as quickly as possible."

I was supposed to come their aid? Mr. Bunting hadn't said anything about this. I may have survived a lightning strike, but that didn't mean I knew anything about reviving a fainting victim.

"...but we feel that you'll feel the way thousands of others do, that it would benefit this or any other city or community if they had the opportunity to witness what you folks are about to. Now you folks that read my articles in *Reader's Digest,* and have seen me on the *Johnny Carson Show* already know the two subjects that I've been noted for all my life, have been juvenile delinquence and sexual relations between husband and wife. However this evening, I hope you will forgive me, I'm going to skip over the juvenile delinquence, and go right into the sex..."

Something about that voice...

A customer came in. "Can I get an Eskimo Pie?"

As the door started to swing shut, I stepped outside.

"...I think most of us already know that too many men enter marriage with a big wise guy attitude. They're big shots, they're big deals, they know it all, and nobody's going to tell them anything. Well the wise guy goes about sex worse than an animal. He does something without realizing it. He builds a hatred, a revulsion in his wife for the sexual act. It usually leads to frustration and nervous prostration on her part. And this marriage usually ends in divorce, because of sexual incapability and ignorance. It's already been proven, my friends, eighty-three percent of women today dread the sexual act because of the way their husbands go about it. I think you know that it's already been proven there's no such thing as a frigid wife, just clumsy men..."

I began walking toward the stage.

"...and I know that you're very anxious to see those remaining medical sequences, and we're going to present them in a few moments, but in the few moments remaining I would like to call your attention to the two books that are edited and distributed by the sponsors of this program..."

"Hey fella, get your butt back to the snack bar! You've got a line of customers waiting!"

"...ninety-nine out of a hundred men I'm sorry to say don't even know that every woman placed on this earth by the good Lord our wonderful Creator was created eight times harder to arouse to passion and reach a climax than a man. That's nothing to be ashamed of — it happens to be Mother Nature's way of working. And it's about time we found it out. This chapter points out, indicates and describes the eight different erotic zones of passion that were placed on every female's body for her husband's use for happy and satisfactory marital relations..."

I passed between the Mustangs and the Corvairs, the man on the stage coming into focus. Wavy blonde hair and cheesy mustache, Clark Kent glasses, accountant blue suit and car salesman plaid tie. He was displaying in one hand a pair of books identical to the library in the snack bar.

"...you know, I've skipped over some important chapters, on venereal diseases, syphilis, gonorrhea and the like, masturbation, how it can be cured, how it can be detected..."

It was Don.

But it couldn't be.

"...the two books are each different from the other, each volume containing thirty-seven actual pictures, drawings, photographs and illustrations. There are some illustrations, and frankly some chapters, that we just do not discuss to a mixed audience..."

Gremlins and Dusters.

I was confused, afraid.

David Prill

What had happened? Where were the hideous girl-crazed monsters? The horror horde of nightmare creatures? Death on the slab?

Where was Dr. Morbid?

And...where was Ronni?

"...I think I've explained everything to you folks tonight to the best of my ability and I'd like to say something about our books. Every place the program plays the management receives hundreds of phone calls and telegrams and letters daily from bookstores all over the country, actually begging and pleading with the management for permission to sell these books to you, the public. The sponsors of this program will not allow them to do it, because I think you know just as well as we do what would happen. They'd put 'em in fancy hard covers all right, and put fancy gold type on 'em and make 'em look real pretty, and then they'd charge you, the public, five, ten or twenty dollars apiece for them. And they'd get it. And the people who'd buy them would be well satisfied, and we don't blame them, because one chapter's worth ten times that..."

He gave up.

Threw in the bloody towel.

"But that's exactly why the sponsors of this program won't allow them to sell these books to you, the public, because of the outrageous prices they would charge. They have made it possible to secure these books right here at this theater, at the cost of printing, binding, shipping and handling. And I guarantee it isn't any five, ten or twenty dollars. It's a price within the reach of everyone. And that price is two dollars per copy, or save yourself a dollar bill and get both books for three dollars. All we ask you do if you'd like to receive them in the privacy of your car, is turn your parking lights on now…"

Lights blinked on, row by row, guiding me to the stage.

"If you'd like to receive them in the snack bar, we will also have a supply of them there. But if you feel you cannot leave your car, turn your parking lights on until an attendant comes to your car, leave them on even after the picture starts, until you have been served…"

I broke into a run.

"…now if you have your money out and hold it in your hand, the attendants will be able to serve you faster and better. So remember, come to the snack bar or turn your parking lights on now, to get your complete set. And now we pause for this brief intermission…"

I stopped just short of the stage. I wanted more than anything to be on a stage with Don — it was where I was meant to be.

But not like this.

Don saw me then, and if he was feeling embarrassed or self-conscious he didn't show it. As always, it was like he had just returned from a trip to the biffy.

"Hey, kid. Give me a hand here, would you?" He passed down the books he had been toting, then awkwardly climbed down from the low stage.

"Don't know what the hell is wrong with me," he said, wincing as he straightened up. "My back has been giving me grief all month." He smiled. "I think all those damn car trips are beginning to catch up with me, you know."

I ached to talk to him, but the words were lost deep in my disappointment.

Don looked me up and down. "You're working here?"

I nodded.

"Good for you. Drive-ins are a gold mine."

I wanted to tell him that I had dug in here on this windswept hillside to await his return, but I just couldn't.

Don scanned the lot, as attendants passed from car to car, collecting the cash.

"Where's Ronni?" I asked.

Our eyes met again. "Look, kid, a lot of things have changed. Why don't you join me for a soda after the show and we can talk."

We headed back toward the heart of the drive-in. Mr. Bunting glared at me as he hustled out of the snack bar, then walked with Don over to the manager's office.

I felt angry, hurt. Don had sold out, let me down.

Didn't he know I was ready?

He had promised...

There are some illustrations, and frankly some chapters, that we just do not discuss to a mixed audience...

Who was he kidding? Mixed audiences had been watching him lop the heads off hapless teenagers for years.

I served up Neopolitan ice cream and delooscious hot doggies in a bitter blur.

I was inclined to avoid him after the show, get in my car and go home and just sink Don and the spook shows into the black bubbling quicksand where most of my attempts at staking out a life for myself had ended up.

But my curiosity won out. I had to know how and why it had come down to this.

And whatever became of Ronni.

And the Twist.

•

"You look a little tense there, kid," Don said as I approached him after the show. He was loading unsold copies of the sex ed books into the back of his Pontiac. Same car, more rust. "What happened to those hopeful innocent Midwestern eyes? It had to happen eventually, I guess. Say, those birth of babies films are scarier than anything in the Horror Chamber of Blood and Doom, don't you think?"

I didn't say anything.

He looked at me uncertainly. "You still up for that soda?"

"Sure."

We went to a Shakey's Pizza not far down the highway. Don ordered a pitcher of beer and didn't offer to share when it arrived. I stuck with a Coke, cherry syrup fortified.

Don took a prolonged draught from his tall glass, a line of suds marking his mustache until he wiped it away, then said, "I knew it was over last fall. The end didn't happen overnight, but it sure seemed that way. I began to notice that the theater managers' ears perked up when I told them about the trashy films I was carrying around, grade-Z gore fests…and that their eyes just glazed over when I tried to pitch them the Horror Chamber of Blood and Doom. The audiences weren't reacting like they used to either. Sending a handful of teen-age boys wearing Don Post monster masks down into the audience doesn't cut it anymore. And bottom line, we weren't the biggest box office night of the week for them. On our best nights, we could match a decent first-run feature. Most of the nights were less than that. They didn't want to be bothered by us anymore. They just wanted to throw the movie in the projector and forget about it."

Don drank again, deeply.

"So I had to eat, you know? Kids out in the sticks are still damned ignorant about sex. I managed to ac-quire a birth of a baby film, reprinted some cheesy sex ed booklets I bought off a guy at a flea market in Joplin, Missouri, gave myself some fancy credentials, and I was in business."

"You weren't in *Reader's Digest,* or on the Carson show?"

"That's just a little harmless ballyhoo, kid. I'm Garganta the Giant Gorilla in horn-rimmed glasses...now I see that look on your face, but think about this: if by attending one of my performances, just one girl in the audience doesn't get pregnant and has a child she doesn't know what to do with, then aren't I doing something worthwhile?"

"But you're a showman. Maybe if you tried some different kind of horror show, found a new angle..."

"Show business is dead, kid. And it ain't coming back."

A guy in a straw hat, suspenders, and a candy-cane striped shirt appeared at our table, grinning insanely, banging away on a banjo.

"So what happens when drive-ins die?" I asked. "One just shut down this spring over on France Avenue. They're putting in a shopping center."

"I can stay out in the boonies. I have no problem doing that at all. That's my core audience anyway." He glared at the banjo man, who scuttled away.

We both worked on our drinks. His pitcher was half empty.

"Aren't you and Ronni..." I began to ask in a quiet voice that didn't have to go far to trail off into a self-conscious silence.

"She didn't make the trip."

"Is she okay?"

"She's doing fine, last time I talked to her. An occasional headache, that's about it. She takes a little blue pill. She was lucky. How about you?"

"I'm okay. I have nightmares about it sometimes, but that's all. I guess I was lucky, too."

Don got down deeper into his beer. "I'm sorry, kid, you know? I wasn't thinking. I was caught up in the show. It almost seemed like the thunder was part of the sound effects tape. Spook shows weren't meant to be performed on the top of drive-in concession stands— maybe that's the lesson the gods were trying to teach us that night."

"So you're not together anymore, you and Ronni."

He gazed at me with eyes that had taken on a far-away glaze. "Not so you'd notice."

"I'm sorry."

"Don't be. She stuck with me through some tough times, and I can't blame her for wanting out. We're still friends."

"What's she doing now?

"She's working for Hubert Castle," he replied.

I didn't recognize the name.

"The circus—riding elephants, or some damn thing," he said, slipping out of the booth, and heading for the Gents room.

At the time I was certain that the circus would come to town, because that's what circuses do. But it never did. Maybe it was a regional promotion. Maybe it was just as well. My memory of her would always be untainted, and I wouldn't be forced to witness the collapse of another American institution.

Don returned a couple minutes later with a fresh pitcher of beer and another soda for me.

"So let's talk about your future," he said, clearly having crossed the border where the pain is numbed to the point of tolerance. "What are you doing with your future? Maybe open your own drive-in someday?"

I dropped my eyes to the table, and batted at the ice in my glass with a straw. I had to fess up. I met his eyes. "The only reason I've been working at the drive-in was so I wouldn't miss you when you came back to town. Because then, see, I could go on a spooker tour with you. It was my dream."

Don felt my pain. I could see it in his eyes. He was still sober enough to feel. Or else my pain was so strong that it cut through the murk in his pickled brain. He nodded slowly, started to say something, then reached again for his glass.

"It was important for me to be at the Lucky Twin," I tried to explain. "It was almost like it was sacred ground or something." I leaned forward. "I've been wanting to run away with your show for so long, ever since that first time I saw you with Dr. Ogre Banshee — you were at the gas station, and the phony corpse was hanging out the back, do you remember that?"

"I remember," he said quietly, and I knew he wasn't just humoring me. He sipped again, then pushed the glass away. "Listen kid, if you hadn't been working at the drive-in you probably wouldn't have been out there tonight, because believe it or not some folks frown on the idea of having anatomically correct posters of the male and female form on every telephone pole and store window in town, you know. What I'm saying is that maybe this was meant to be."

Now he met me halfway across the table. "Kid, I've been seriously thinking about adding a second sex ed unit. I'm not bullshitting you. I could train you in the pitch. It's all scripted — there's nothing to it. You have a real sincere manner about you. We could head down south. You'd get every hillbilly down there to turn on the parking lights on their jalopies."

"You're a huckster."

"I'm making a living. That's the way the world works, kid. Pitch 'em sodas or beer, soap or sex. It's all the same. People will try to be polite about it, pretend like they aren't trying to get you to wave your dollar bills out your car window. But it's all the same."

"It's not all the same. You loved the spook show business."

"Not healthy to love a corpse. I wouldn't recommend it."

"This isn't exactly what I had in mind."

"It's the most I can offer you."

"I know."

"Look, times change, fads come and go, people forget, and then they remember. Maybe one day the world will get so nasty that folks will need a few goofy monsters and stunts to see them through. We'll be a nostalgia act."

"And until then, it's skipping over juvenile delinquence and going right into the sex."

"Hey kid, I like the way you say that!"

•

We left Shakeys and Don drove me back to the Lucky Twin to get my car.

We shook hands, wished each other good luck, and parted ways.

I never saw Don again.

I just couldn't do it.

I didn't want to sell twenty-five cent sex ed books to hillbillies for two dollars. And I didn't believe that spookers would ever come back into fashion, even as nostalgia, and I don't think Don really believed it either.

I was ready, at last, but I was too late.

It was a profoundly helpless feeling.

What I didn't know at the time was that Don had tied his dreams to the drive-ins so thoroughly that when they went belly up he had no way out. I heard that toward the end he even produced a series of no-budget gore films for the drive-in circuit, and did okay for a couple years until mainstream Hollywood discovered how much money was in chronic evisceration.

Don was right: show business was dead.

I could see the changes in my town, too. Everything was becoming jumbo-sized, voluntarily regimented, habitually impersonal. My whole childhood world had disappeared, replaced by chain stores, office parks and townhouse hives, like some cut-rate Kara-Kum magic trick.

What chance did a guy in a rust-chewed Pontiac and a suitcase full of spook paddles have in this world?

So how did Dr. Morbid die?

It wasn't the alcohol.

He was thrown off the stage, one dream at a time.

Until there was nothing left of him.

Until he was just a luminous hollow-eyed figure seen in a dark hall, flitting above the heads of the audience before blacking out forever.

Introduction to
Children of the Carp

Now the truth can be revealed, to you, the chosen few:

I owe my writing career to a fish.

Not just any fish. Not a trout, nor a walleye, nor a muskie, nor any other of the highly prized trophy fish that inspire wet dreams in the minds of most Minnesotans.

A carp.

A bottom-feedin', bad-eatin' nuisance fish who typically finds itself on the wrong end of a flailing boat paddle.

But without our friend the carp, there would have been no *Serial Killer Days* — and my life might have turned out very, very different indeed.

Back in the late 1980s I had been typing words on plain white 20 lb. paper off and on for years with no success. I was ready to give up, give in, and get my city planning degree (what kinds of cities would you plan? an old pro once asked with amusement and fear). I had never workshopped, and literally had no contact with any other writers or would-be writers, but somehow in 1988 I hitched up my nerve and applied to a well-known summer writing program at a large Midwestern land grant university.

My application was rejected.

I knew it was just a misunderstanding, so I applied again the following year, and that summer I found myself haplessly thrashing about in a stifling dorm room, trying to find that elusive "voice" the writing teachers droned on about. I might have been hearing voices anyway. It was really hot.

Finally, just as the big ivy-choked doors of summer were about to close, I banged out "Children of the Carp" (whose original title, if my memory serves me correctly, was "The Carp of Wonder"). It got a mixed reaction, but I didn't care. My gut said I was onto something. I had been trying to write offbeat, small-town, Andy-Griffith-Show-on-acid fantasies, and during the creation of "Carp" I finally figured out that by mixing Mayberry with a twist of darkness I could produce something pretty darn volatile.

So, how did "Children of the Carp" become *Serial Killer Days*? Simple: you have all your life to write your first novel, and a year to come up with your second one. After *The Unnatural* was unleashed, to good reviews and tepid sales, I wrote virtually an entire novel that I had to abandon (somehow combining a homicidal President of the United States and a high school girls wrestling team—don't ask). In a prime panic, I dove into a pile of stories, everything I had written, trying to find something, anything that I could dig my nails into...

Ahhh. My friend, the carp.

I thought I could simply expand on the main concept and make a decent book, but it didn't seem to be quite right. How about narrowing it down to just one of the ideas in the story? Yeah. I didn't want to jettison the Carp of Wonder, but I had to. It was the only way. Sorry, big fella.

I'm amazed and thrilled that "Carp" is finally seeing publication, in a hardcover with a slipcase no less. I appreciate the opportunity to share with you this little piece of myself that has been hidden for so many years. Writing is often a mysterious process, but if someone asks me "Where did it all begin?" I can hand them this book, this story, this fish, and say "Here."

Children of the Carp

Ever hear of Meteor Days in Bluesoon, Nebraska? How about Chewing Gum Days in Wiskatama, Wyoming? Or Mosquito Days in Lumbertown, Minnesota? No? Then you probably aren't familiar with the career of Thornton Puckett, unknown genius behind many of the rites and rituals and celebrations which have been the salvation of small-town America over the past forty years.

Thornton Puckett lived with his son Nick in a modest white house in Nestberg, Iowa. The bookshelves, tables and countertops abounded with trinkets and oddities brought back from his many trips across the country: plastic footprints from Bigfoot Days (Grainyville, Washington and Loopid, Oregon), a rubber chicken from Rooster Days (Running Foot, Wisconsin), a plastic hot dog garnished with plastic relish and plastic mustard from Wiener Days (Atlantis, South Dakota), and multitudes more.

The most sacred object in the house was the rubber carp reclining in quiet dignity on the coffee table. Thirty-five years ago, Carp Days in Goodness, Iowa had saved the town from bankruptcy and launched Thornton's career.

Today was the big day in the Puckett home. Thornton had decided, after weeks of deliberation, that it was time to leave the road and devote himself to his sunflower garden. It was also time to pass on the secrets of his craft to the next generation. That meant his son Nick, a dark-eyed dropout from the Philosophy Department at Iowa State. Thornton couldn't stand the frantic music the boy played on his stereo, but thought he had a fine brain and a real knack for creative thinking.

"Son, are you sure you want to follow in your old man's shoes?"

"There's not much we can be sure of in this life," Nick mused, poking thoughtfully at a hole in the plaid sofa. "Our existence is so ephemeral, so ultimately meaningless."

"But in the context of our conversation," Thornton said, having learned how to cope with Junior since his enlightenment, "what would your answer be?"

"In that context, the answer would be yes. Definitely. It would appear to be a real chance for expanding my consciousness."

"You know, sonny, there's a lot more to the business than this consciousness stuff." He picked up his treasured souvenir from the coffee table. "There's a lot of...rubber carp, if you know what I mean."

"Even a rubber carp has a unique place in the universe."

Thornton grinned. "That's my boy! Now, the first thing you need to know is how this sucker works. On the one hand you've got a town, preferably a town that's going downhill—businesses have closed, people are moving out. City officials are looking for anything that will bring bucks back in. Got it?"

"Of course."

"On the other hand you've got companies who are only too eager to get some free advertising. Did you know that Carp Days was sponsored by a fishing-tackle manufacturer? And that Bigfoot Days was brought to you in living color by a camera-film company?"

"No, but I think I could have offered a reasonable conjecture if you had given me a moment."

"Sorry, son. You can answer the third part. Where do we come in?"

"As facilitator, I would assume."

"That's right. The first task is to choose a town. Takes a lot of research in the library, a lot of phone calls. The next step is to go to the town. Walk the streets, talk to the people, learn the history. Step three is finding that something special which sets a town apart. Every town has one. Carp, harmonicas, giant balls of string, you name it."

"I find that highly unlikely," Nick said. "The homogenization of American culture is one of the great crimes of the twentieth century."

Thornton sipped some lemonade, thinking of a riposte.

"But," Nick added, "no town would ever admit it."

"Son, your mind works in strange and wonderful ways. Don't change a single brain cell."

Nick smiled slyly. "What's next on the agenda?"

"The easy part. The pitches, both to the town and to the sponsor. If you've done your homework, it'll be like sliding down a greased, uh, lightning rod. Then you organize, promote the heck out of it, and hopefully watch the magic happen. Any questions?"

"Not in the sense you mean."

"In that case," Thornton said reverently, "I present you with the rubber carp." Tears spattered the back of the sacred fish as he passed it over. "Make me proud, sonny boy. Make me proud."

Thornton taught Nick the ropes over the next few weeks, the father-and-son team barnstorming across the Midwest, from Dinosaur Days in Chillimick, Kansas to Peanut Butter Days in Groupmind, North Dakota. While it was tempting to keep the partnership running, Thornton stayed true to his word and retired in late June.

The first letters and phone calls Thornton received from Nick after their split were encouraging. While Thornton knew that his son was riding his coattails, he hoped that by the time the Puckett name no longer carried its weight, Nick would be well on his way to establishing his own reputation.

It was on a humid Saturday morning at the end of July when the bad news came. Thornton had been working in the sunflower garden since dawn, digging weeds and whispering words of encouragement, and was taking a lemonade break when the phone rang.

"This is your son."

"Hiya, pal. How did Waffle Days go?"

"They went."

"Where are you now?'

"Crowface, Kansas. Future home of Dogfish Days. Population unknown. Elevation unknown. Reason for my being here unknown."

"What's wrong, son? You sound a mite gloomy."

"I have been bitten by the spider of boredom."

"Bored? How could you be bored? You've got the greatest job in the world. Ask anyone."

"Another town, another dumb fish."

"You're just lonely and homesick. I went through the same thing when I first started. Try to stick it out for awhile, okay?"

"I will give it eight days, not including today."

At three in the afternoon the following Sunday, Thornton ran in from the sunflowers to answer the phone.

"Hello?"

"Hello."

"Nick? Is that you?"

"My dreams are becoming strange, Pop. I keep dreaming I am living in a town where every day of the year is Carp Day. All the restaurants serve nothing but carp. The streets all are named carp — Carp Street, Carp Avenue, Carp Drive, Carp Lane, Carp Circle. The mayor's name is Cyril Carp. In place of Washington on the quarter is a carp."

"Where are you now?"

"In Togo, Minnesota. At Crabapple Days. Carp don't like crabapples, do they?"

"Why don't you drive home tomorrow? You should see how high my sunflowers are getting."

"Well, actually, I believe my consciousness has been expanded to all practical limits in the carpticular arena."

"Are you saying you want to quit?

"Actually, yes."

Thornton felt riled up. He moved away from the window, so that the sunflowers wouldn't be showered with the bad vibes.

"You listen to me, sonny boy! When I started out in this business, what kinds of Days do you think towns had? I'll tell you! Worthless, trivial, boring crap! Brown Shoe Days! Pots and Pans Days! Paperclip Days! Days were nothing before I came along! I was a pioneer, an innovator, the Einstein of Days! I know you respect your old man, but by God you must rethink, remodel, and reinvent the whole damn thing! Tear me down! Rip me apart! Make the Days over in your own image! It's not carp the restaurants are serving, it's Nick Puckett! The streets aren't named carp, they're named Nick Puckett! It's not a carp on the quarter, it's Nick Puckett! You can do it, sonny boy! You can do it!"

From the other end of the line came the sound of crashing furniture and a simian-like screeching, translated into something like, "Yah! Yah! Yah!"

A week later Thornton received a letter from Edgar Lever, the mayor of Standard Springs, Wisconsin. Thornton had briefly worked for the town several years ago on the Chipmunk Days project, walking out when the politicians tried to take over creative control.

Dear Mr. Puckett:

I am writing this letter to express my extreme displeasure at the actions of your son, Nicholas Puckett, whom we hired as a consultant to assist us in developing an idea for an annual event. I am

*speaking both for myself and all the members of
the city council when I say we were deeply offended
by your son's suggestion that Standard Springs
stage something he referred to as Dead Dog Days.
I will not go into the details here. Some of us still
have a sense of common decency. Needless to say,
we expect an immediate apology.*

*Sincerely,
Edgar Lever*

Thornton felt somewhat concerned, but held no sympathy for the Standard Springs power brokers. He went outside and watered his sunflowers.

Two days later a phone call came from Madeline Grest, mayor of New Olds, Minnesota.

"...and when we asked him for his recommendation, he told us that after careful study he thought we should hold Malaria Days. Now if this is a joke, I don't think it's very funny..."

The trail wound on, from Minnesota to the Dakotas to Nebraska.

Sewer Rat Days.

Flag-Burning Days.

Necrophilia Days.

Stand Up For Satan Days.

Thornton gnashed his teeth in the sunflower garden. He hadn't heard from Nick in weeks. *I've created a monster,* he thought, clutching at the dry stalk of a sunflower for comfort. *My reputation is ruined. The Days will return to the Dark Ages.*

One morning a package arrived by special delivery. It was from Nick, with a return address at the Thrifty

Digs Motel, Highway 5, Goodness, Iowa. Thornton ripped apart the packing paper and dug through the Styrofoam peanuts, hoping to find some explanation for his son's erratic behavior.

What he found instead was the rubber carp.

Thornton tried to keep calm, tried to remind himself that Nick was just an out-of-control kid, but to see that carp, the symbol of all his fatherly trust, was too much for him to bear. He saw Nick's face on the carp, mocking him, daring him to accept the challenge. The boy needed to be taught a lesson.

Thornton discovered the traitor in the lobby of the motel, casually smoking a cigarette and reading a newspaper. How arrogant can you get? he thought, running past the desk. Thornton tore the paper from Nick's hands and started whacking him about the head with the carp.

"You ungrateful brat! How could you do this to me? How could you do this to yourself?"

"Your presence here is unfortunate," Nick said, dodging the blows as best he could.

"Isn't it enough to trash my good name? Do you also have to spit on our sacred trust?"

Whack, whack.

"Are you referring to the carp?"

"The passing of this carp was the greatest moment of my life! I thought it meant something to you!"

"But you told me..." Nick said, and then the chair tipped backwards and the struggling pair tumbled onto the coffee-stained carpet. Thornton landed on top.

Whack, whack.

"For crying out loud, son, do you realize what you're doing? Necrophilia Days? Stand Up For Satan Days? Are you insane?"

Nick finally grabbed his father's arms and said quietly, "I am a success."

Thornton stared at him in disbelief. "Don't give me that. Those towns ran you out on a rail."

"Initially, yes. But my concepts, my art, has struck a nerve in contemporary small-town America. I have three projects already accepted, and offers from all over this plugged-in country of ours."

"Never! Never in a million years!"

"Perhaps not in a million years. But this year, yes."

"Show me."

"If you wish. You may not like what you see."

"Show me."

It was walking distance to Goodness. They strode along the shoulder of the road in silence, dust from the gravel swirling behind them. Thornton cradled the carp like an injured child.

Reaching the edge of Main Street, they stopped. A black banner had been hung between the streetlights.

SERIAL KILLER DAYS - August 21-28

"It is going to be the event of events," Nick said, admiring the sign. "Exhibits will chronicle the lives of the most renowned serial killers in history, with an emphasis on the modern era, of course. The carnival will be unique and thrilling, featuring rides such as the Open Bedroom Window, the Back Seat, and the Parking Ramp at Midnight. The highlight of the week is going to be on Saturday evening, with a pig roast followed by the Parade of Fear. The only problem I anticipate is with the parking."

"How?" Thornton asked numbly.

"Nothing ever changes. Yesterday's carp is today's serial killer. The town fathers aren't interested in content, only numbers. All I did was serve the client."

"This...this was my town. It made me what I am today."

"And it will make me, too."

What have I done? Thornton lamented, looking with despair at the rubber carp. What have I done?

The first Sunday of September was crisp and bright, a hint of fall in the air. Soon the killing frost would take the sunflowers for another year. Thornton tried to spend as much time as he could in the garden, bonding with the flowers, making their last days as enjoyable as possible.

"Finest crop of sunflowers in my lifetime, Pop."

"A good year, but not the best," Thornton said, keeping his eye on the water streaming from the can. When the water began pooling around the base of the plant, he tipped the can upright.

He had expected Nick to show up and gloat, and Thornton found himself unable to look at his son. "So, how did the, um, thing go in Goodness?"

"Turn-away crowds. We had to bus people in."

"Um, great. Where are you off to next?"

"Sniper Days, in Biggertown, South Dakota. I believe I've found my niche."

Thornton set down the can and looked at his son squarely.

"You know, Nicholas, I shouldn't be blaming you for this. It's in the nature of things. I should be proud that you chose to follow in my footsteps. Who knows, maybe the guy who thought up Paper Clip Days got mad when I showed up."

"Are you still mad at me, Pop?"

"'Course I am. But it'll pass. Maybe one day I'll understand what you're doing." He laughed. "Don't know if I got enough days for that, but I sure will try."

Nick touched his father's arm. "If I ever choose to procreate, I hope I can be as good at parenting as you are…"

●

Years later, with many successes behind him, Nick decided it was time to leave the road and devote himself to writing offbeat philosophical tracts. It was also time to pass on the secrets of the Days to the next generation. That meant his daughter Nicole, a bright-eyed graduate of the Iowa State School of Business…

●

"Preferred Stock Days? Corporate Merger Days? Are you insane?"